# The Amazing Mind of Alice Makin

# From The Chicken House

I've always loved those old films where children run wild in the city all day, making friends and lives of their own in secret places. In this story the secret places are inside the kids' heads, and the things that happen there are more strange than anything that happens on the streets of their home in old war-torn London. Stand by to be puzzled and amazed!

Alan Shea beautifully fuses the real and the imagined like no one else – perhaps you'll think more carefully about what you wish for in future…!

Barry Cunningham
Publisher

# The Amazing Mind of Alice Makin

ALAN SHEA

2 PALMER STREET, FROME, SOMERSET BA11 1DS

First published in Great Britain in 2008
This edition published 2014
The Chicken House
2 Palmer Street
Frome, Somerset BA11 1DS
United Kingdom
www.doublecluck.com



Cover design by Steve Wells
Typeset by Dorchester Typesetting Group Ltd
Printed and bound in Great Britain by
CPI Group (UK) Ltd, Croydon, CR0 4YY
The paper used in this Chicken House book
is made from wood grown in sustainable forests

1 3 5 7 9 10 8 6 4 2

British Library Cataloguing in Publication data available.

ISBN 978-1-909489-87-5
eISBN 978-1-909489-91-2

*For Margaret, who'll always be my Alice.*
*For my mum and dad.*
*For John and Patrick, my sons and best friends.*
*For Cerys, Alice Theresa and Steve.*
*For Barry, Imogen and Anna.*

# ★★★ 1 Beginnings

I see it like I'm a camera: distant, apart. I'm in class. It's break. I look down on to the playground. Focus on Reggie, the new boy. He doesn't fit in. He's different somehow, and the others know it. I feel sorry for him.

He's watching wasps that have nested in a wall. They come and go, in and out of the tiny hole, in an endless rhythm. A procession of life. He watches them. I watch him. Zoom in . . . snap.

The playground backs on to a canal. Its surface shimmers. The sun burnishes the water gold. The glare blinds my eyes. September sings a song only it knows; summer's swansong. Soon be over. Days grow shorter, nights grow longer.

I'm twelve. It's my first year at senior school. Miss Druce, our teacher, is leaving, going to look after her dad. Don't think of teachers as having dads. I help her take her life out of the cupboards and pack it into boxes. Dismantle her years here. Take things off walls that look as if they've been there for ever.

Soon the room is bare, a tattered tree in autumn. Miss Druce doesn't say much, but every now and then she stops and lingers too long over some old photo. Wipes her eyes on the hanky she keeps up her sleeve.

Outside, Reggie's still watching. The wasps are his world. A moment in time: frozen. He's wrapped up, oblivious to everything else. I'm not. The Spicer twins have seen him. They walk towards him. Not directly – slow and sly. Winding like snakes. I push open the window and Denis's voice drifts up.

'Cor, look who's here, it's s-s-stuttering Stanley.' He twists his lips. A dark smile.

Gary Spicer laughs. Worms his hands deep into his pockets, 'Or is it r-r-r-rattling Reggie?'

Denis moves closer. 'Read any g-g-g-good b-b-b-books lately, R-Reggie?'

He exaggerates the stutter, machine-guns the words. They both laugh.

'Or had any good bloody noses?' Gary shoves his fist under Reggie's nose. 'What you lookin' at there?'

Reggie stands in front of the wall, tries to shield the nest. Too late.

'Ah, look. It's a lovely little wasps' nest.'

Denis Spicer takes out an elastic band from his pocket, loops it over his index finger and thumb and pulls back the elastic. He aims at a wasp, lets go. 'Oops. Me hand slipped.'

The elastic band dissects the wasp. It oozes life. Crawls crippled. Gary Spicer takes chewing gum from his mouth and sticks it over the hole – locking the door on the nest.

Other wasps return; they maze, confused. Exposed. Denis snaps the band wickedly, snapping bodies. Reggie looks down on the floor at the dead wasps and tries to understand. He can't. He turns to walk away.

Gary blocks him. 'Where d'you think you're goin', Titch?'

Reggie's answer sticks in his throat. Judders to his lips. Spurts out. 'N-n-nowhere.'

'Yeah, good place for you, mate.'

Laughing, they grab him. Pick him up like he's a baby. He doesn't struggle, just lies still. The high wire fence that keeps us from the canal is broken in the corner. It comes away easily. They carry him towards the hole.

I say to myself, 'Don't let them push you around, Reggie. Stand up for yourself.'

Gary has him around the neck, hitting him on top of the head with the palm of his hand as if he's not worth hitting properly. They pull back the fence and make a bigger hole. Reggie's glasses fall off. Denis treads on them. Crunches the glass.

I clench my teeth. Grit out the words, 'Hit him, Reggie. Give him something to remember you by.'

'What did you say, Alice?'

'Nothing, Miss.'

I know he won't fight. My words die in the dusty classroom. Laughing, they push him through the hole. Pull the wire back. Shut him out. Close the door.

Reggie gets up. Brushes the dirt off. Looks back

through the wire. He says something. Denis doesn't like it. His face changes, the smile is wiped off. He pulls open the wire again, and starts to climb through. Reggie sees him coming: freezes.

I can almost hear his brain working. This is a problem. Behind him is a deep, dirty canal; in front of him, Denis. To his right there's a long towpath that leads to the bridge. I'm not sure if he knows it, but if he takes the towpath he can get to the bridge, then up the steps to the main road.

I screw up my mind. Concentrate. Try to send him the message. Go right, Reggie. Go right. Luckily, that's the way he goes. I decide to try and help him.

I walk quickly past Miss Druce. She looks up.

'Where are you off to, Alice?'

'Nowhere, Miss. Won't be long.'

'Don't be. The bell's going soon.'

As I get to the door she goes to the window to see what I've been looking at. I go quickly down the stairs and out of the main gate, head up Copenhagen Place and turn left into Salmon Lane, going towards Commercial Road. This will lead me straight to the bridge. I run as fast as I can. The streets are fairly quiet, so no one gets in my way. By the time I get to the bridge, my heart is pounding. I stand there catching my breath. I've got a stitch in my side.

I can see Reggie in the distance running down the towpath towards me. He's managed to keep ahead of Denis, but only just. Every now and then Reggie looks back. Denis is gaining on him.

I take a deep breath and start to go down the steps that lead off the side of the bridge and down to the towpath. I take them two at a time, wondering as I go if I'm really doing the right thing here. Maybe I should let him fight his own battles. After all, I've not known him that long. Anyway, what's the worst Denis can do? Thoughts dance through my mind in time to my feet as I fly down the steps. If this was the Olympics and there was such a thing as step dancing, I'd have just won a gold medal!

I reach the bottom. Stand with my hands on my hips, my head down, panting, trying to suck in air. My heart has turned into a sledgehammer trying to knock its way out of my chest.

They're a few hundred yards away; they haven't seen me. Reggie's concentrating on not getting caught, Denis on catching him. The canal towpath used to be concrete but it's been neglected. Now it's a ragged mess of stones and mud. Reggie's foot goes into a pothole. He stumbles but doesn't fall. Denis shouts something, just as a lorry thunders by on the bridge. I don't hear what he says. Reggie's legs are pumping, but he's slowing down. It's like he's gone into slow motion. His brain's saying, '*Run*', but legs don't have ears.

Denis is almost on him now. I start to go towards them. I once had a fight with Denis – he won, but I gave him a bloody nose. I'm not scared of him and he knows it. Mind you, he's tough as old boots. The trouble is, so is his brain. He's getting closer. Reggie seems to put on a spurt, pulls away a bit. Denis shouts again, and this time I hear him.

'You're gonna go in that canal when I catch you, you little freak!'

Reggie stumbles. His legs wobble. They're stuttering, just like his words. Caught up in themselves. He falls. Denis is almost on him. I bite my lip. I'm never going to reach him before Denis. He'll make mincemeat out of Reggie.

Why is it the good people always get it? Wouldn't it be great if, just for once, things evened up a bit in life? Like it was the Spicers who were being chased for a change. A cross between a dragon and your worst nightmare snapping at Denis, growling, baring its teeth.

Then this strange thing happens. Denis stops. He's just standing there. He's not even looking at Reggie, he's looking at something else. He's staring up at the sky behind me. His mouth is open, his eyes wide. He looks scared: his face ghost-white. Reggie is still on the ground. He sits up. Looks across to where Denis is looking, then his eyes slowly go to me.

Denis begins to back away, almost stumbles. Then he turns and runs, heading back towards school like the devil's after him. Must be the first time Denis Spicer has ever run to school in his life.

Reggie gets up, and rubs at some blood on his elbow. Then he looks at me again with a strange expression. Makes me shiver.

## 2 Me and Reggie

Monday. November. Bright and cold as a packet of pins. I walk home from school, whistling. A weak winter sun leaks into the sky. Charcoal clouds smudge out the blue, rubbing out colour as if the sky is a drawing gone wrong. The air is smoky; tastes of bonfires. Mist on a stick. Have a lick of autumn.

I live in this block of houses, three storeys high. Bit like flats. Some people call them tenements. Mum calls them slums. We live on the ground floor. I go in, walk down the passageway. The passage is open to the street and the only way in and out for everyone who lives there. 'Like Piccadilly Circus that passage,' my mum says, 'never know who you're going to meet.' The floor is stone, the walls flake paint. It's always cold.

I call out as I go past the one bedroom where we all sleep and walk towards the one room we all live in, 'Mum? Where are you?'

She calls back, 'I'm in here.'

The voice comes from the bedroom. I stop, go back and in. In the room are two beds separated by an old curtain. Mum and Bert sleep in the one near the door. I sleep in the one over by the window. Mum's sitting on her bed mending a hole in the sheet.

'Anything to eat, Mum?'

'"Hello" would be nice.'

'Sorry.' I say it slowly. 'H.e.l.l.o. Mum. Anything to eat?'

'Don't be a clever-clogs. For that, you can wait.'

I watch her sewing.

'How was school?'

'All right. I got into a bit of trouble with Miss Lacey.'

'Why?'

'Talking. She said I must have given Sheila Morgan an earache.'

Mum smiles. I sit on the bed.

'I got a prize from Sister Bernadette for my story.'

'Another one?'

She says it a bit like I've told her I've got toothache.

I go to a Catholic school. It's called Our Lad's. Well, it's not really called Our Lad's. It's Our Lady's. It's just that the 'y' went missing off the sign on the school gates – the Spicers probably nicked it to use as a catapult.

The school is run by nuns called the Sisters of Charity. The Sisters wear hats. They're stiff as a board and they sweep up on either side of their heads into wings. Flying nuns – now that would be something to see!

I write stories. I'm not a swot, I just like doing it. Making things up. Making people up. Once, Sister Bernadette, she teaches English, found one of my stories inside my English book. Said she liked it. I got embarrassed. Sometimes she looks to see if there are any more. Occasionally I slip one in. Nice to be told you're good at something. Doesn't happen that often.

'So, what did you write about?'

'Dunno. I can't remember.' I can, but I can't be bothered to go into it. I want something to eat. I fish in my pocket. 'She gave me this.'

It's a little white plastic statue of the Virgin Mary. On the way home from school I put it under my jumper, and it glowed. 'It glows in the dark.'

Mum looks up from her sewing. 'That'll be all right when we run out of shillings for the electric meter then, won't it?'

She's trying to be funny. When my mum is trying to be funny, she has this little smile on her face like she's laughing at her own joke which only she understands. She looks up. Looks at the statue.

'It's lovely.'

'Mum?'

'Yes, love?'

'I think I need glasses. When I'm concentrating hard on something I get this funny dizzy feeling in my head.'

She pulls a face. Re-threads the needle.

'You probably need to go to the lav.'

'Mum. It's in my head.'

''Spect it's your age then, love. You'll grow out of it.'

I once heard Mrs Gilbey tell Mum she had a pain in her

back and a bad shoulder and Mum said, ''Spect it's your age, love.' At least she didn't say, 'You'll grow out of it'. Just as well, as Mrs Gilbey is seventy.

'And how's Reggie been?'

She asks the question casually. Like she doesn't really care. One eye on me, one on the sewing.

I've seen quite a bit of Reggie since the start of term. Trouble is, Bert doesn't like him: says he's a 'bad lot'. I said, 'A bad lot of what?' He clouted me for being cheeky. It was worth it though.

Mum knows I like Reggie, so she gets caught up in the middle. She said the other day that she felt she was the rope in a tug of war, with me pulling at one end and Bert at the other.

'Alice, stop daydreaming. I asked you how Reggie is.'

'Dunno.'

'Don't say "dunno"; it's common. Anyway, what d'you mean you don't know? You spend enough time with him.'

'You can't tell with Reggie. He don't say a lot.'

Reggie lives in the flat upstairs. There's him, his granddad and Flash. Flash is his dog.

Reggie doesn't go to school much. Even when he's there he just sits looking out of the window most of the time. Miss Druce liked him. You could tell. She used to keep an eye out for him. Sat on a cushion to see over her desk. Sweet as sugar and sharp as an acid drop. Strict but fair. Worried at us like a sheepdog worrying sheep, nipping at us with a glance or a word. The Spicers didn't mess with her. She wasn't very big, but her stare was. She had this way of making her voice just loud enough, her stare just hard enough.

'Denis Spicer, I saw that.'

'But, Miss . . .'

She full-stopped the Spicers. 'Leave. Reggie. Alone.' End of sentence. End of story. Miss Druce was water, putting out their fire. She didn't shout or anything. Just *sssssssshhh* on the flame. The Spicer twins extinguished.

She understood Reggie straight away. Most people don't. She only taught us for six weeks, but I'm sure she knew us all.

It all changed after she left. Miss Lacey is nice too, but different. She's young, soft skin, white blouse, bright smile, expectation in her eyes, uncertainty in her voice. She doesn't seem to see things: the crafty elbow in the ribs, the kicks under the desk, name-calling, embarrassment, hurt feelings.

The Spicers don't like new boys, they do their best to make Reggie's life a misery. Nothing very dramatic, they never were original. They take the mickey, hide his things, write rude words on his books, that kind of stuff. They pick on him because he won't fight back.

Although I'm friends with Reggie, they leave me alone. I've got a bit of a temper – goes with my red hair. Mum says I chose to be his friend so that I could protect him. 'That's the way you are, darlin', God help you,' she said.

I love my mum, but sometimes she doesn't know what

she's talking about. I liked Reggie from the start. He doesn't try to be something he's not. He's just himself and you either take him or leave him. That's the way he is. Trouble is, there are a lot of people out there who won't let you do that. Reggie just likes being outside and making things. He's brilliant at that, he can make anything. Except a friend.

Mum bites off the thread. 'They're a strange lot.'

'How d'you mean?'

I can see her looking at me. She doesn't really know. But that's part of the thing with Reggie, you know what you feel but you don't know why.

'Well, for a start his granddad's not his real granddad, you know. He's just looking after him. Even the dog's a bit scatty. And . . . well . . . there's just something about that boy I can't put my finger on.'

Her eyes rest on my shoes. 'You been scuffing the toes of your shoes again?'

'No, I fell over.'

'I'll give you fell over.'

I wonder what 'I'll give you fell over' is supposed to mean but I don't say anything.

'You won't get any new ones until Christmas, you know.'

'Roll on Christmas.'

'Don't you be so cheeky, my girl.'

I get up. I keep the things Sister Bernadette has given me on the windowsill near my bed. There are quite a few there now. I'm proud of them really, although I pretend I'm not. Maybe I'll be able to read a comic under the bedclothes later by the light of the luminous Virgin Mary. Then again, maybe not. I go to put the statue with the rest of my prizes. Can't see them. That's strange.

'Mum. My things have gone from the windowsill.'

She looks up. There's something in her voice.

'Oh, they're over on the chest of drawers.'

I go over to the drawers, knowing there's something wrong.

My treasures are all messed up, a wreck of paper and plastic. The holy picture's ripped. A rosary broken; beads scattered. Some things are missing. I don't say anything because I know what's happened.

'Your dad must have knocked 'em on the floor by accident.'

Mum calls him my dad but he isn't really. He's my stepdad. I think of him as Bert, not Dad. That's his name, Albert Makin. Bert's what most people call him. He doesn't like me writing or reading or drawing or, come to think of it, doing just about anything – except clearing up; that seems to be all right. He's always complaining that I'm cluttering up the place with all my 'junk' from school.

'Why can't he just leave my things alone?'

I can feel Mum looking at me, though she's pretending not to. 'Oh, you know what he's like.'

I do, but that's an excuse, not an answer.

I clear up the beads and torn paper. I feel a bit upset so

I go out to the back yard. It's quiet out here. I sit on the wall. Wait for the feelings to pass.

Out here everything still looks a mess: it's ten years since the war, but bombs leave deep holes in the ground, and even deeper holes in people's lives. There are empty spaces where there used to be houses, empty places where there used to be people. I look across to the bombed ruins – torn-apart buildings that used to be homes. On walls open to the sky, wallpaper flutters. The ghosts of mirrors linger in neat, clean empty squares.

From where I'm sitting I can see up to Reggie's window. A light comes on. A shadow passes behind the curtain. I wonder what did happen by the canal? That was a real mystery.

'You there, Sherlock?'

'Yes, dear girl.'

I sometimes talk to Sherlock Holmes when I've got a mystery that needs solving.

'I was just wondering, about the canal that day. You're a great detective.'

'Wouldn't argue with that.'

'You can solve any mystery. What d'you reckon happened?'

He lights his pipe, thinks for a long time, puffs out a cloud of smoke and says, 'Haven't got a clue, dear girl. Not a clue.'

'Well, almost any mystery.'

# ★★★ 3 Stepdad or demon?

Morning. Light squeezes thinly through the curtain. It's freezing cold in the bedroom: my sleeping breath is iced into lacy patterns on the window. Layers of frosty me. I scratch my name into it. It's Saturday. Funny how it's easier to get up when you're not going to school.

My clothes drape over the chair, cold and stiff, waiting to come back to life. I put them on, go through the old curtain that Mum put up to separate my space from theirs, then out the bedroom door.

I walk down the passage and into the front room which is also the kitchen. We call it the front room, but it's the only room besides the bedroom, and it's at the back not the front. Suppose we should call it that, really. But 'the only room besides the bedroom at the back' would sound stupid. So we don't.

There's an old gas stove, a sink, a table and two chairs. It always smells stale, feels cold, looks bare. I turn on the tap over the sink; it chugs like a train, then gurgles out a stream of brown water. I let it run until it gets cleaner. No one's watching, so I only have a quick wash. A lick and a promise, Mum calls it. I roll my collar down, attack the tide mark.

On the draining board are a few dirty plates. A saucepan of leftover porridge – a bit burned. My mum's not exactly the best cook in the world. She's better at burning things. Her bread pudding is great, though. I could live on her bread pudding.

I sit at the table and eat straight out of the saucepan with the biggest spoon I can find. Dig out the porridge – concrete that hasn't yet set. It tastes of smoke. I ice it with sugar.

While I eat, I notice there's another patch of mould growing on the wall. At this rate there'll be more mould than wall. If I squint, it looks like a ship – a tall ship, with sails of peeling plaster, floating in a sea of green fungus. There's another patch that looks like an angel. I decide to write a poem about an angel sailing a tall ship in a sea of green fungus. I get my out my old biscuit tin, that's where I keep my stuff, and take out a pencil and an exercise book. Now, let's see what rhymes with angel and fungus—

The door opens. I know he's come in. I don't look up. Sometimes I think it's better if I just don't look at him. Bit like I'm pretending he's not really there. Or maybe I'm pretending I'm not really here.

'What you doing? Day dreaming again?'

He goes over to the sink and starts to run the cold water. He puts his head under the tap. Scoops water on to his face from cupped hands. Sucks it into his mouth, pumps it around noisily. Spits it out into the sink.

'Always wasting your time.'

'I'm writing a poem.'

'You're writing rubbish.'

'It's not rubbish, it's about a . . .'

'I don't care what it's about. Get those books off the table. Now!'

I don't argue. There's no point making him mad. He scowls, looks across at Mum, then seems to remember something.

'And another thing, mind you keep away from that good-for-nothing upstairs. I saw you with him again the other day. He's trouble. D'you hear me?'

He glares at me, daring me to argue.

'Yeah. I hear you.'

But I think, 'Yeah, I hear you. Doesn't mean I'm going to do it though, does it?'

He looks at me sharply, almost as if he's heard me. He's got these eyes that sort of drill into you. They're cold and flat but sharp as needles all at the same time. It's like he can see inside my brain. I stare at the floor. He makes me feel uneasy sometimes, as if he knows more about me than I want him to. I can't help wondering sometimes what my real dad would have been like, especially when Bert's in one of his moods. I think my real dad would have been different. He would have helped me, been proud like real dads are, even when you're not really that good at something. They're just proud of you because you're you. How great is that? I know it sounds mad but sometimes when I think of my real dad I get this feeling. It's peaceful, like someone's stroking my face with a feather.

Bert's voice cuts into my thoughts.

'What time did you come in?'

'It wasn't late.'

'I didn't ask you if it was late . . . '

He lays his trap.

' . . . I said, what time?'

I fall into it.

''Bout six o'clock.'

'Well, that's too late. You can stay in tonight – clear the place up a bit.'

No matter what time I'd told him, he'd still have said the same thing.

I don't argue. He sits watching me while I eat my breakfast. I collect some of the dirty things from the table and take them to the sink. I can feel his eyes on my back. I let the water run on to the dishes and the saucepan for a while.

'And don't leave your stuff all over the bedroom. Rubbish, that's what it is. Like the rubbish in your head.'

I know I shouldn't answer him back, but I can't help it. I hear myself say, '*It's not* rubbish. They're the prizes I got for my stories.'

He gives me that look again. Although I'm half expecting it, it always surprises me. He takes one step towards me. I pull back. Too late. His hand smacks me around my cheek. It stings like someone has just splashed boiling water on my face. I want to put my hand to the spot; but I don't; I don't want him to see that it hurt. I want to look at him. To let him see how I feel. Without words. Let him see it in my eyes.

'Not so clever now, are you?'

He takes out his tobacco tin. Rolls a cigarette. Lights it. Blows blue smoke. Stares back at me.

'You and your stupid stories. Just a load of old lies.'

'They're just my stories.'

He smirks. Proves his point.

'Stories are made up; if they're made up, they're not true, and if they're not true . . . ' He pauses. Stabs me with the words. 'They're just a load of old lies.'

He looks hard at me, daring me to say something.

I know better. Best to get out. I go back out into the passageway. To the right is the toilet. I walk past that and into the back yard. Mum's out there singing as she hangs out the washing.

'I'm going out, Mum.'

She looks over at the window. Lowers her voice. 'If you're going with Reggie, mind your dad doesn't see you. He's in one of his moods today.'

I could see Bert didn't like Reggie from the start. I think he'd rather I was friends with the Spicer twins. And he doesn't like them at all.

'And if you do go out, don't go over where the old people's places used to be. They were knocking them down yesterday. Don't want you coming home with a broken neck.'

I want to say, if I broke my neck I wouldn't be coming home, but I don't. 'I'll be all right.'

'Never mind about that. Don't go over there. D'you hear?'

I go back into the passage. As I do the front room door opens. Bert is standing there, waiting to see what I'm doing, making sure I don't go up for Reggie. His cigarette curls grey smoke. He narrows his eyes. Looks through the haze. He takes a final puff, then flicks the glowing end into the air. I walk past as quickly as I can.

## ★★★ 4 Up the stairs

I make my way down the passage, open the bedroom door and slam it hard as if I've just gone in there. But I don't go in. I wait for a while in case he's still watching. After a few minutes I take a chance. Go back down the passage to the old staircase. There's no sign of him, so I creep quietly up the stairs to Reggie's. We agreed we'd start collecting wood for our bonfire today. I'm looking forward to that.

It's a damp, dark wooden staircase. Smells like it's got hundred-year-old armpits. But to me going up the stairs is always an adventure. Sometimes it's an equatorial rain-forest full of amazing birds and swamps and giant creepers. Sometimes it's a space ship like that thing on the wireless, 'Journey into Space', and I'm the captain and we're on our way to the stars. But today I think it can be . . . I know . . . a snow-covered mountain. Yeah, great. Deadly ravines, walls of ice. I'm a mountaineer, climbing Everest without oxygen. *Is there no end to this girl's bravery?*

I make it up the first flight. The air is thinner up here. I look over the banisters. A blizzard is drifting in. What do I care? Have a gob-stopper, they're full of energy. Scientific fact. I push on. Each step at this altitude is painful, but I have to go on. I'll be the first girl to climb Everest, then go out to collect wood for bonfire night in the same day. Sensational.

Then I see it, lumbering down the mountain pass. It's huge – at least ten feet high. Evil, staring eyes. Covered in fur. It eats human flesh, and it's heading straight towards me. It's the Abominable Snowman. It opens its mouth and lets out a blood-curdling roar—

'Morning, Alice. Still talking to yourself, I see.'

'Morning, Mrs Cassidy. Not all the time.'

'Glad to hear it. How's your mum?'

'She got eaten by a snow leopard on the ice face.'

'Shame. She was a good woman.'

'Yeah.'

'Better keep off the ice face today, then?'

'I should, if I were you.'

'Righty-o.'

'Oh, and watch out for avalanches too.'

'Mrs Thompson hanging out her washing on the landing again?'

'It's like a snow blizzard. Could be nasty.'

'Does that mean I've got to ski round her husband's underpants again?'

''Fraid so, Mrs Cassidy.'

'Oh well. Live dangerously, that's my motto. Must get on. I've got to pop down the butcher's at base camp. Get some chops for tea.'

'See you, Mrs Cassidy.'

'Bye, Alice.'

I watch her go. Everest turns back into boring old wooden stairs. I take them two at a time. They creak out their age. Darkness seeps from the walls, clings like a leech.

I'm at the door. Knocking for Reggie is dangerous – Flash is a rocket! The sound of a knock launches him, and when the door opens he detonates on your legs. Reggie says he's only guarding his territory. I say, yeah, and I'm only guarding my legs. So I climb over the banisters, keeping the wooden rails between me and Flash. I lean forward and knock.

My knock echoes back. No barking. No Flash. Perhaps there's no one in. But then the door slowly opens, and Granddad's head appears round the door. He's notched and gnarled. Blue eyes like a stream with the sky reflected in it. His hands are veined like the rivers on the maps at school. His hair is snow-white. His teeth have fallen over each other in his mouth, as though in a rush to go somewhere. My mum says he's lucky to have his own teeth. I wonder who else's teeth he's likely to have. He smiles when he sees me, not one of those smiles that some people slip on and off but like he means it.

'Ah, it's you, Alice.'

I like his voice. It's soft. Lots of adult voices have got edges on them. Like if you don't do what you're told they'll get their voices on to you: knock you out with a crafty sarcastic uppercut to the jaw, get you with a shouting kidney punch, a telling-off right jab. Granddad's hasn't got an edge, though. No angles. No sharp corners.

'Reggie in, Granddad?'

'He's out over the debris. Said to tell you. He's getting the cart ready to go. You're collecting wood for the bonfire, aren't you?' He chuckles. 'Never seen him so excited.'

'Thanks, Granddad.'

I go back down the stairs, creep past our door and outside to a crisp-as-toast morning. The day is glad to be out of bed. It's looking forward to itself.

Reggie's sitting on his cart. Flash is over by the old air-raid shelter, digging. Reckon Norman must have been training him to look for unexploded bombs. Suppose we'll know if he finds one.

Reggie made the cart himself from some planks and the wheels off an old pram. It's even got a brake. He's looking across the debris, staring as if he can see something miles away. Fingers of oil pattern his cheeks. His collar's rucked up and a bit frayed at the edges.

The sticking plaster on his glasses is peeling off like the opening page of a book. Reggie's got a lazy eye. This doesn't mean that it lies around all day in a deckchair doing nothing. It just means that the muscles in it are weak. He has to have sticking plaster over his good eye to make his lazy eye work harder.

I call out: 'Wotcha.'

'You t-took your time. I've been waiting ages.'

'Well, you could have waited a lot longer. I wasn't going to come out at all.'

'I knew you would.'

'No you didn't.'

'I d-did.'

'What, are you a mind reader or something?'

As he straightens up, his glasses slip down on his nose. He wrinkles it to stop them falling off completely. His eyes go to my cheek and he looks at me funny.

'What you staring at?'

'You've got a r-red mark on your face.'

Instinctively my hand goes up to it. His eyes narrow, like he knows.

'Looks like someone's h-hit you.'

I change the subject. 'You don't look so great yourself. Your hair's all sticking up. What d'you do, comb it with the leg of a chair?'

He spits on his hand, rubs it over his blond hair. It springs back immediately.

'Was it your stepdad who h-hit you?'

'Who said anyone had? Anyway, you want to mind your own beeswax.'

'He's a bit sort of s-scary.'

I lie. 'I'm not scared of him.'

He looks at me for a while, like he's trying to make up his mind about something. Then his eyes change and he grins.

'D'you l-like my jumper?'

'Now *that's* scary.'

It's a zig-zag jumper; zig-zagging colour across his chest. Looking at it makes my eyes go zig-zag too. A rainbow of wool. Captured from the sky and knitted.

'Looks like you've been struck by lightning, mate.'

He tugs at the neck.

'Feels like it. It itches like m-mad. Norman's m-mum knitted it for m-my birthday. I hid it in the drawer. Thought she might forget about it. '

'Did she?'

'No. She asked Granddad when I was going to wear it.'

He nods, points to one of the wheels of the cart.

'P-put your finger there.'

I do. He tightens a nut.

'That's got it. C-come on, then. You g-get in and I'll pull you across the road. Test it out. It's got to take a lot of weight if we're going to collect loads of wood. Pity you're skinny.'

'Slim. Girls are slim.'

He pushes his glasses back up his nose. Wrinkles it.

'Sorry. Right. Jump in then, skinny.'

I stick my tongue out, just to show how grown up I am, and jump in. Flash looks up, realizes something's going on, and he's determined it's not going to go on without him. He comes over. Gets in the way. Jumps in the cart. Starts barking like if he does it loud enough the cart will go.

Reggie gets some string out of his pocket. He's always got bits of string. He's a collector of bits of string. There's a bit tied on to the front wheel that you're supposed to steer with. Trouble is, it's the long bit that he normally uses to keep his trousers up. So he can't pull very fast, not with one hand holding up his trousers.

It's a good cart. He made it from bits of old wooden boxes we found in the ruins opposite. You have to be careful where you sit though, there's lots of nails still sticking up. Granddad gave us some paint, but not enough. So now it's a bit red but you can still see 'Property of the Co-op' showing through. One wheel doesn't fit too well either. Still, nothing's perfect.

'R-ready?'

'Let's go.'

'Indian territory?'

'Wagons roll.'

We wobble around the streets. Pretend we're cowboys. The West is wild. We're wilder. We scout for wood. Pick over the bones of bombed houses we shouldn't be in. Sort through the rubble. Pile in as much wood as the cart will hold. Then, when the wheels start groaning, we take off. A wagon train chased by Indians. Flash becomes Big Chief Crazy Dog. Runs behind, barking out war cries. Takes no prisoners. Tries to nip our legs.

We escape up the broken staircases of bombed-out buildings. Fire out of windows. Winchesters and six-guns blaze. They've got us surrounded. After our scalps. After our wood. But we're too good. They flee in a hail of bullets and dynamite sticks. Mothers with prams look up, smiling.

We wobble back through the streets, taking it in turns to be the horse. Make our way back to our debris to unload. Slowly we turn the untidy piles into a giant pyramid. This is going to be a bonfire to end all bonfires!

I look up. The sun's a yellow ball kicked high in the sky – if it was a rugby ball and the horizon was the crossbar, it'd be a goal. I can just see the newspaper headlines: *God gets scorching last-minute drop kick with the sun.*

'Is Granddad going to help set the bonfire up?'

'D-don't know. Why?'

'Just wondered. '

I'm really looking forward to it this year. It's one of my favourite times. The smell of the smoke. The noise and colour of the fireworks.

'It'll be great having our own bonfire. We can roast some spuds in the embers. I'm goin' to ask Veronica Silk, George Morgan, Norman and that lot. What about you?'

He starts to pile up the wood into a wigwam shape. 'I'll ask Granddad.'

'I'll ask Mrs Gilbey, then. She can keep him company.'

'Who?'

'That lady you met last week. You know, we carried her shopping.'

He looks blank.

'I told you about her. She used to look after me when I was a little girl.'

'Oh, yes.'

'She likes you.' I try to embarrass him. 'Called you that

"nice young man". Must have got you mixed up with someone else.'

It's supposed to be witty, but Reggie takes no notice. I try again. 'You never know, they might become friends.'

Reggie picks up one end of a great big piece of wood. It's dirty; got horrible green stuff on it. Looks like a manky old tree trunk.

'You've got to be joking. I'm not touching that.'

He looks at me, surprised. 'I d-didn't ask you to.'

'Yes you did.'

'No I didn't.'

'Must be hearing things then. Here, d'you reckon if Mrs Gilbey and Granddad become friends they'd go over the park together?'

'Maybe she'd c-cook him some dinners.'

'Yeah, and Granddad could help her around the house.'

'Maybe they'll f-fall in l-love and get married.'

'You could be bridesmaid. She'd make you comb your hair.'

He grins.

The sun is an orange, leaking juice into the sky. On the grass, dew winks back the light. Spiders knit glistening webs, crochet bushes, spin light. You can hear the silence. It feels good sitting here with Reggie, looking forward to things.

He takes out a half-eaten packet of Refreshers, undoes it and tips a rainbow of colours into his hand. Spreads the sweets out.

'There's a few mauve ones left. I s-saved them f-for you.'

I take one.

'Why do you l-like the mauve ones?'

''Cos they taste like they look.'

He puts a Refresher into his mouth. Sucks it.

'Here, I know what I was goin' to ask you. That day at the beginning of term, remember? Denis Spicer was chasing you down by the canal? He had you in his sights, then he stopped dead like he'd seen a ghost or something.'

'What about it?'

'Just wondered why he stopped.'

Reggie bends down. Starts fiddling with a piece of wood. I can see he doesn't want to answer.

'I don't know. Maybe he thought he'd be l-late getting back.'

'What, Denis Spicer worried about being late for school? You must be joking.'

'Maybe he r-realized that I'd smash him to smithereens.'

'You and whose army?'

He waves at someone behind me. I hear the sound of machine-gun fire. Then Norman's voice.

'Oi! You two. Surrender or die.'

# ★★★ 5 Norman's knitted underwear

He's sitting on the back of his dad's milk cart, coming towards us. It pulls level. Norman grins at Reggie, recognizing his mum's zig-zag handiwork. 'Nice jumper, mate.'

Norman's mum likes knitting. He's got knitted scarves and jumpers, ties and socks. I wouldn't be surprised if he wore knitted underwear. Norman wants to join the army when he leaves school. If he ever does, I reckon his mum will knit him a uniform. Even his face looks like it's been knitted, although she must have dropped a few stitches here and there because his mouth is too big and his ears stick out a bit.

Norman's dad sits at the front of the milk cart. Flicks his whip at Daisy the horse without ever touching her, although her flanks twitch in anticipation. Mr Higginbottom still wears his army trousers, even though he left the army ten years ago. Norman always wears his camouflage jacket, though he's never been in the army at all. And Daisy has an army beret perched on her head, with holes for her ears. She's never been in the army either, but Norman once said that she was in the Horse Guards. As a joke – at least, I think it was – you never know with Norman. He yells across to me.

''Ere, Alice, I've just shot your mum.'

I shout back, 'Her singing's not that bad.'

'She's sending messages to the enemy with her washing. Two pairs of knickers on the line, that's a signal to attack.'

Without turning around Norman's dad says, 'Watch your language, boy, or I'll tan your bloody backside for yer.'

Norman sticks his tongue out at his dad's back, then takes aim and puts a bullet in it. Point blank. Points his rifle at me. 'How do I know you're not German spies too?'

''Cos we go to the same school as you.'

He ignores this. Fires. I duck. Funny how you do that – duck imaginary bullets from a wooden rifle.

'Tell your friend Veronica to meet me at the gasworks tonight. I'll be wearing me new army belt.'

'All right, Norm . . . in your dreams.'

'If she doesn't turn up, you die tomorrow. Firing squad at dawn.'

'Any particular reason?'

'Failing to obey an order.'

'Sorry, Norm. I'm busy at dawn tomorrow.'

'Me t-too.'

'I can make it Tuesday.'

'Right – don't be late then.'

Mr Higginbottom calls back something about Norman shutting his big gob. Flicks the whip. Daisy sighs, strains at the harness.

'See you in school on Monday.'

'See ya.'

Norman is still firing, this time at a bunch of German spies disguised as sparrows. I watch him turn the corner. Daisy's hooves ring into the distance and die.

# ★★★ 6 Bonfires, bother and . . .

'Look out!'

Mile End Underground station empties, a volcano spitting lava people. A gloomy afternoon. November grey. Streets full of people too busy talking to notice us. I try to get out of the way. Can't.

Then they notice. Start moaning. 'Kids . . . under your feet when you don't want them. Never find 'em when you do.'

We fight the current of suits and bowler hats, overalls and raincoats. People plodding, sour-faced. But we don't care. We've important things to do. We're heading for Giovanni's shop to get our fireworks.

'It's going to be a great fireworks night.'

'Amazing.'

'F-fantastic.'

I sense a battle. 'Brilliant.'

'W-wonderful.'

'Amazing.'

'You've h-had that.'

'All right. Tremendous.'

He pauses. 'Incr-credible.'

We cross sluggish traffic. Cars cough. Limp lazily to a stop at traffic lights. Breathe cloudy fumes. Mist on mist.

I try to buy some thinking time. 'Good film on at the Odeon.'

He's not having it. 'I w-win.'

'No, you don't. I was just saying there's a good film on at the Odeon.'

'Only to give yourself t-time to think of a word. The rule is, you *don't* think.'

Unbelievably, a word slides in.

'All right. Unbelievable.'

It's as we turn into Victoria Park Road that I catch sight of them out of the corner of my eye. My heart sinks, splashes annoyance.

Reggie's still playing.

'S-superb.'

When I see the Spicers I'm immediately on the alert. Somewhere in my head, a blue light flashes. A siren whines. My hand tightens on the money in my pocket. We've collected five shillings, taking our Guy Fawkes dummy around the streets. It was a really good one – it's amazing how realistic a few sacks stuffed with newspapers, dressed in one of Granddad's old waistcoats and one of Mum's old hats can look. Mind you, I don't think the real Guy Fawkes would have had an old nylon stocking around his neck to keep his stuffing in. Five shillings is a lot of money. We've split it – half a crown each.

'You got your money?'

'Get on with the g-game.'

'I give up. You win. Now, have you got your money?'

He nods.

'Well, hold on to it. The Spicers are over the road.'

The Spicers are as broad as they are tall. If they joined Norman's army they'd be the tanks. Push and Shove. Tight eyes. Tight lips. Crew cuts. Even their hair looks dangerous.

They're busy with something. Got their backs to us. They huddle together. Bodies as shields.

'What they d-doing?'

We should really walk straight past, get out while the going's good. Mind our own business.

'They're trying to get gum out of that machine without putting any money in.'

'How d-do you know?'

'I've seen 'em do it before.'

It looks like they're succeeding. As we watch, their pockets begin to bulge and the bubble gum machine starts to empty.

'W-what shall we do?'

'Just mind our own business?'

'Or w-we could stop them.'

'And get thumped.'

'Depends how w-we do it.'

'Got any suggestions?'

'W-we could t-tell the shopkeeper.'

'And get thumped.'

'Or w-we could draw attention to them.'

'How?'

'Simple.'

He cups his hands to his mouth. Shouts. Loudly. 'W-what you two d-doing?'

Denis spins around. Furious.

I glare at Reggie. 'Oh, great, we're gonna die trying to save a bubble gum machine.'

Denis looks over at us. Draws a finger across his throat. Looks up and down the street. Sticks his hands in his pockets and whistles with what he thinks is an innocent look. Couldn't look more suspicious if he tried. Gary kind of sidles off, as if he's nothing to do with Denis. Which, considering they're twins, is a bit stupid. Gary looks over. Makes a rude sign. I make one back.

'What gets me is that they always get away with things.'

'Kn-know what you mean.'

'If we do the slightest thing wrong we get into trouble. They seem to get away with everything.'

'It's n-not fair. Come on, best leave them to it.'

I stare at them, thinking all kinds of nasty thoughts. Wishing something would happen. Imagining how good it would be if they got caught, or ended up with more gum than they knew what to do with.

A big lorry roars by; blocks our view for a second, shakes the pavement. When I next look, something amazing happens. The bubble gum machine starts to sway slowly backwards and forwards. Then it tips right over and hits the floor, shooting out bubble gum in a torrent of colours.

The Spicers look amazed. I wouldn't have believed it could have held so many. Scattering out. Pouring out. A sea of bubble gum balls. The twins check no one's watching, then start scooping it up. Handfuls of it. Stuffing it into their mouths, and, when their mouths are stuffed, stuffing their pockets. Seems the more they stuff, the more it comes. They've got enough gum to last them until they get their pensions!

Still it comes. Building up in waves around their feet. They start to tread on it – I can hear the thin sugar shells cracking. Gum meets shoes. Gum sticks to shoes. Spicers stick to pavement. It's hilarious. Looks like someone has poured glue all over the floor. The look in their eyes changes from glee to confusion. Bubble gum pulls out in long tacky strands as the Spicers try to lift their shoes. They're both well and truly stuck now. Denis reaches down and tries to take off his shoe, but his fingers stick to it. He's tied up in bubble gum. The more the twins struggle, the more they get caught. It's the funniest thing I've seen in ages.

Me and Reggie get the giggles. They both look across at us. Don't look very happy. The Spicers don't like being laughed at. If they knew what the word 'revenge' meant, it would be burning in their heads, branding their brains.

Instead, the words 'Knock their blocks off' are probably doing the burning. Whatever, we need to get going quick before they get unstuck.

'Better leave the fireworks for today. We'll get them tomorrow.'

'G-good idea.'

I can't resist another look. The gum is still pouring out. How much can one of those machines hold?

'That was great. Wonder what made that gum machine fall over like that?'

'Yes, I w-wonder.' Reggie's voice sounds strange. Almost like he's teasing me.

I glance across at the Spicers. Denis gives me a filthy look. It's time we were gone.

'T-tactical withdrawal?'

'What?'

'That's what N-Norman would say.'

'No, he'd say leg it.'

We head out of the street as fast as we can, and around the corner.

'Know what?'

'What?'

'Those Spicers are d-dangerous.'

'Dodgy.'

'Dastardly.'

'Dastardly?'

'It's a real w-word.'

'Desperate.'

'Desperate?'
'Fancy seeing that film?'
'Stop cheating.'
And so on. Down the road we go.

# ★★★ 7 . . . bad feelings

It's bonfire night. The sky drizzles. Overhead, dumpling clouds dish themselves up in a school-dinner-gravy sky. And I've got indigestion in my heart. Me and Reggie have had a row. Well, not really a row. It was more me being horrible to him. I'm like that sometimes. 'Cut your own throat one day with that tongue of yours,' my mum says.

I'm standing under an oak tree in Victoria Park. Vicky Park, we call it. I've decided to get Reggie a peace offering. He told me he'd seen a really good dead branch hanging from this tree the other day. Thought it would be perfect for our bonfire. Thing is, he can't stand heights. So I thought I'd go and get it for him. Peace offerings are supposed to be olive branches, I think, but we don't get many of those around here. He'll have to make do with a bit off an old oak tree.

I like climbing. Being at the top of the world. Hanging in the air. On my own. I look up at the tree; should be easy enough. I grab hold of a small branch, wrap my legs around the trunk and start to climb. There are plenty of hand-holds, so I soon zoom up.

Out of the corner of my eye I see something. I look

down. It's Norman. He's creeping up in the cover of some bushes. He's got some twigs stuck in his hair. I can't make out if it's supposed to be camouflage or he's just forgotten to comb it. He wriggles on his belly to the foot of the tree like some giant, knitted caterpillar. Stands up and cups both hands around his eyes like he's got a pair of binoculars. Army issue, of course. He looks up at me.

'Oi, Al, wotcha doing?'

'Escaping from Colditz, Norm.'

He adjusts the binoculars. 'Good on ya. Can't see no Germans.' He swivels his hands. 'I could see up your skirt though, if I wanted to.'

'Not if you had a black eye, you couldn't.'

He turns away. 'Right. Get your point.'

Trevor Taplin's mum comes into the park with her dog. Norman focuses his binocular hands on her.

'Here, Al, d'you reckon Mrs Taplin is really Adolf Hitler in disguise?'

Wish he'd shut up. I'm nearly there. Trying to concentrate.

'No, I think Mrs Taplin is really Mrs Taplin, Norm.'

'How d'you know?'

'Well, I think if she wasn't, Mr Taplin would have noticed by now, don't you?'

'Suppose so. Mind you . . . '

He pauses. Thinks. I'm at a tricky bit. Got to reach out to grab the dead branch.

' . . . she has got a funny moustache like Hitler.'

I try to reach and talk at the same time.

'Yeah, and your dad's horse has got a funny walk, but that don't make her Charlie Chaplin.'

'Right, get your point.'

'Watch out, Norm!' I let the branch fall. He moves. It misses him – just.

'Mind you, that's because she's gotta pull a milk cart. You'd walk like Charlie Chaplin too if you had to pull a milk cart round behind you all day.'

'Expect I would.'

Now I've got to get down. Have to make sure I've got a good hold on the branch above with my hands before I let go with my legs.

'You know if you fall you're gonna break your neck?'

'Not if I fall on you, I won't.'

He carefully puts the binoculars he doesn't have in a case he hasn't got.

'Hey, you seen the Spicers lately?'

For a second I look down. Nearly miss my footing.

'No, why?'

'They've been feeding our goats the *News of the World.*' Norman's dad keeps goats and chickens in the little garden at the back of their bungalow.

'My dad said they'd get food poisoning.'

'Who, the Spicers?'

'No, the goats. Anyway, what d'you want with an old dead branch?'

'It's a peace offering.'

'You're a fruitcake, Al.'

'Takes one to know one, Norm.'

'Your mum'd kill you if she knew what you was doing.'

He's right. One slip up here and . . .

I start to climb back down. That's really easy. Just like sliding down a pole. I get to the bottom branch, jump off.

'Thanks, Norm.'

'What for?'

'Oh, nothing.'

'That's all right. That's what I'm good at. Nothing. That's what my dad says. "Know what you're good for, boy? Bloody nothing, that's what."'

I leave Norman laying mines and looking for German snipers near the swings. I drag the dead branch out of the park and down Burdett Road. Get some funny looks. There's two blokes standing at a bus stop. One looks at his mate like he's going to say something really witty. Then he says, 'See you're branching out on your own then, love.' And falls about laughing. I stick my tongue out. Walk past.

It's getting dark already when I get back to the bomb site. Rain falls heavily from the foggy autumn sky. This is where our secret camp is. Well, not so secret really – just the old air-raid shelter. I stack the branch next to the rest of the wood. Duck inside the shelter.

I come here a lot to think, or sometimes just to get away. It's falling down in places. The old, rusty corrugated tin roof's fallen off and some of the bricks have crumbled.

The floor is just earth. But me and Reggie have made it all right. We've stuck up some old canvas as a roof to keep the rain out, and we found some milk crates to sit on.

I keep my stuff in here now, out of Bert's way. My writing books, pencils and my Sherlock Holmes books are all in an old biscuit tin. I've had it for ever, ever since I can remember. I asked Mum once where it came from. She said it was a special present and she'd tell me why one day. On the lid is a picture of a girl with red hair, bit like me really. The picture is difficult to see now, because the lid's pitted with red rust spots and a bit faded. The girl is sitting on a swing, looking out across a field. There's something on the ground near to her but I can't make out what it is. There's the maker's name on it but it's all been scratched so I can't read it, and next to it is written 'Best Biscuits' in this lovely curly writing. I wonder if they do one with 'Worst Biscuits' written on it too. One end of the tin is crumpled so it doesn't fit any more. It looks like someone trod on it. Someone did. My stepdad.

I'd been trying to write a story. I was lying on the floor, had my stuff spread out around me. He bent over and nudged my elbow so that my pen left a streak of ink across the book. Then he laughed and slowly trod on the tin lid. One end just folded in. Squashed. I didn't know why he did it. Still don't. Maybe he guessed how much I loved it. For some reason, it always makes me think of my dad.

Mum never talks about my real dad. I used to ask her about him but she always got funny. Like she had to be on her guard. She'd always put me off.

'Another time, Alice, I'm too busy at the minute.'

or

'Tomorrow, love. I'll tell you about him tomorrow.'

And guess what? Tomorrow never comes. Seems strange that she doesn't want to talk about the man she loved, the man who was the other part of our family. That makes me sad, especially when I look at my stepdad and see the kind of things he does. Like he's trying to show me something, to let me see that he's bigger and stronger than me, that he's the boss. Thing is, if he really loved me he wouldn't want to boss me around.

# ★★★ 8 Fireworks

I settle myself on one of our old milk crates. Rain hurries down as if it can't wait to leave the sky. Drums its fingers on the canvas roof. I was hoping Reggie would be here. Hoping we could make it up.

I look out at the branch from the tree and think about our row. It started because I had to go and do an errand for my mum, so I gave Reggie my money to get the fireworks. He bought them at Giovanni's sweet shop. Put them on his cart, then went next door to get something for Granddad. He saw the Spicers hanging around, but didn't think anything of it. If it had been me I'd have thought a lot about it. For a start I'd have thought the Spicers and unattended fireworks don't go together. In fact, the Spicers and anything unattended don't go together – even your unattended granny. If it's not nailed down, they'll pinch it. If it is, they'll just pinch the nails first.

When he came out of the shop the fireworks were gone. The whole box – five shillings' worth. I had a real go at him. He was upset. Said he was sorry. Most people would have left it there. Not me – I told him to get lost, and he went. Razor tongue strikes again. I felt awful. Maybe one day I'll think before I open my big mouth.

I'd been looking forward to tonight for ages, as well. Dreaming of all those lovely fireworks. Now all we've got between us is a couple of packets of sparklers and bad feelings. I told the other kids I'd invited from school we'd lost the fireworks. I thought it was only fair. Most of them said they wouldn't bother to come over just to see a bonfire. They'd go and find some other street with a bonfire *and* fireworks. George said he'd try to get over later. Veronica said she'd do whatever George did. I said she should make up her own mind. I was a bit disappointed with Veronica. We're good friends. But then, she does like George.

Oh, well. Suppose I'd better swallow my pride and go and find Reggie.

I'm about to get up.

'Alice?'

He whispers my name as if he's afraid of it. I get up too quickly and bang my head on the canvas roof. Water shoots off. He peers around the corner.

'Thought I'd f-find you here. Me and Granddad thought we'd g-get the bonfire ready, if that's all right with you.'

Flash pokes his head in between Reggie's legs. Looks really funny, like he hasn't got a body. He must be the nosiest dog in the world; always has to know what's going on. He sees me and barks. I'm really glad to see them, but I'm going to act as if I'm not really bothered.

'What about the rain? You'll never get it to light in this.'

'There's just a few m-more bits of wood to stack. By the

time we've finished it might have stopped. You going to h-help?'

I duck out. Look around. Like I'm making up my mind. Really, it's already made up.

'Yeah, I might.'

'Come on, it'll b-be great.'

'I got you another bit of wood.' I point to the branch I got from the park.

He grins. 'B-blimey, I thought that must have been dropped by a giant b-bird building a very large n-nest.'

'Reggie.'

'What?'

'That's not funny. And don't say blimey. It's common.'

'You say it.'

'That's different.'

He smiles. So do I. Never was any good at being angry. Life's too short, Mum always says.

'F-friends?'

'Friends.'

'Let's g-get going then.'

'Won't be a minute, I've just gotta get Mrs Gilbey. I promised I'd call for her when we were gonna light it.'

He moves aside to let me out, brushes my arm, accidentally on purpose. Flash runs around barking. Starts digging in the dirt.

'Sorry that I w-went and left the fireworks where the Spicers could get them.'

'That's all right. I'm sorry too.'

'I've got a f-feeling it's going to be a really good bonfire night.'

'You reckon?'

'Yes, I do.'

I look up. Don't think the weather agrees with him. The rain starts to drift in heavy, flat sheets, cold and grey against the sky. If it keeps up it'll spoil everything. I walk to Mrs Gilbey's, really wishing it would stop. Start singing 'rain, rain, go away, come again another day' like I used to when I was a kid.

Mrs Gilbey's house is only across the road from the bombed debris, so it doesn't take long, but by the time I get there I'm soaked. The lamp in her window throws a blur of cream light through the curtains. I knock. It seems to take her an age to answer. The door opens. Light spills out on to the pavement, pulls her out with it.

'Hello dear, nice to see you.'

'Sorry I've not been round for a while, but things got a bit complicated.'

'Don't they always. Everything all right now?'

'Yeah. I've come to get you for the bonfire.'

'Not going to put me on it, I hope?'

I laugh. 'Not straight away.'

'Cheeky.'

'We've not got any fireworks, though. Reggie . . . well, they sort of got lost.'

'Never mind, love. A bonfire is fine. Can't beat a good bonfire.'

'Granddad's gettin' ready to start.'

'Right, we'd better go then.' She looks up. 'You might have a bit of a problem getting it to light in this rain, Alice. Blessed nuisance. I'll just get a headscarf.'

I step in and wait for her. She goes to a drawer and takes out a pretty red and gold headscarf.

'There. I feel quite excited. Ready?'

She offers me her arm and I slip mine through hers. She feels warm, and smells of lavender soap and cake. She's safe and strong. You know she won't let you down.

We step out into the night. She pulls her coat around her. It's a nice coat – fawn colour, with a big wide collar she turns up around her face. We huddle against the drizzle.

I really wish the rain would stop. Why can't it be a bright starry night? I can just see it, a clear blue-black sky fuzzy with stars. Just the night you want for a bonfire. The thoughts in my head turn. Wrap around each other. I imagine the best firework display in the world in a clear night sky: rockets and bangers and Roman candles and spinning Catherine wheels.

Mrs Gilbey looks up and holds out her hand to catch raindrops. Looks puzzled.

'Goodness me, it *is* stopping. They said on the wireless it'd rain all night. Oh well, maybe they'll get it right one of these days.'

I look up into the darkness. The sky suddenly clears. Stars prick, wink a million winks. How great is that.

'Must be your lucky night, dear.'

When we get to the debris, Reggie and Granddad have already got the bonfire lit. Mad sparks tear off like fireflies, scattering into the sky.

Granddad piles on more wood. I wave to him. His face flickers shades of red, caught up in the glow of the fire. He has his penknife out and is sharpening the end of a stick.

'Reggie's just gone to get some potatoes to roast. We forgot to bring them.'

He stops. I can see him looking at Mrs Gilbey, wondering who she is.

'Granddad, this is Mrs Gilbey.'

The flames light up his face. 'Good evening to you, ma'am.'

'Mrs Gilbey is . . . ' I don't know what to say.

She helps me out. 'A friend.'

Granddad smiles. Makes a kind of bow and holds out his hand. 'Pleasure to meet you. Angus Macdonald.'

I nearly laugh. That must be his name. Mrs Gilbey shakes his hand.

I hear Flash barking. He sees me. Comes running up, wagging his tail, nosing around. His tongue is a flannel; gives my face a wash. Then Reggie appears out of the darkness, carrying an old shopping bag. He sees us, waves and smiles.

Granddad takes the bag and shakes out five huge potatoes. 'Now for the feast, eh?'

He turns to Mrs Gilbey with a big smile. 'Would you

like to join us? You'd be most welcome.'

She smiles. 'That sounds very nice, Mr Macdonald. I'd be delighted.'

Granddad takes one of the potatoes, puts it on the end of the stick and slides it into the embers. He does it again until there are four potatoes roasting. I can almost taste them already.

As it gets darker the fire gets brighter. The flames take hold. Fingers of fire caress the wood. Magicians' fingers, coaxing it into flame. On top of the bonfire the Guy's clothes shrivel in the heat. The warmth of the fire hugs me. I can feel its heat on my face, taste the smoke. It gets into my eyes and makes them water. I can smell it on my clothes.

I look round at Reggie and Granddad and Mrs Gilbey. It's funny, a while ago I was thinking things couldn't get any worse. That they'd never get better. Shows how wrong you can be. Standing here is the best.

The bonfire collapses in on itself, spits and hisses at us like some angry dragon. Other people, attracted by the fire, begin to drift across. Granddad rakes over the white-hot diamonds of wood. They burst into flames as he touches them.

I'm hungry now. I look at the jacket potatoes. Reggie fishes one out and gives it to me.

I break it. Let it cool. Steam folds into the air; smells great. My tummy waters. My mouth says 'wait for me'. The sweet white inside blisters into flavour on my tongue.

Granddad takes out a small piece of newspaper, twisted into a spiral, filled with salt. He offers it around. This is great. Being here in the cold and dark, crunching into our potatoes. The only thing missing is the fireworks. But at least we've got our bonfire, and you have to be grateful for what you've got, Mum says. That's only common sense, because you can't be grateful for what you haven't got, can you?

I start thinking about how brilliant it would have been to have had our own fireworks. I imagine the noise and the colour and the sky alight with flaming stars . . .

A rocket splits the darkness. Explodes in the sky. Out of the blue. Out of the dark. Unexpected. It makes me jump. Another launches, so close I can feel it as it sears past me. It tears the darkness, shedding a silver spray, shredding a path upwards through the sky. Then another. Their paths dissect and cascade into a pattern of light and sound; beautiful music that patters down on our heads like singing rain.

I call out, 'Look at that!'

Granddad sucks in his breath.

'Well I never.'

Mrs Gilbey sighs. 'They're beautiful!'

It's just what I imagined our fireworks would be like. The best! Only thing is, we don't have any. But they're coming from somewhere. Lots of them. The night explodes. Firework colours paint the night: red, blue, green, silver, gold. The sky fizzes; wriggles and writhes with a life of its own. Rockets whisper secrets upwards. Bangers crack like rifles. Mrs Gilbey looks up into the night.

'You are a tease, Alice. I thought you said you didn't have any?'

'We didn't . . . at least, I didn't think we did.'

'Well, it's a lovely surprise.'

Firework follows firework. Tail-chasing, star-gazing, sky-blowing, mind-filling fireworks.

'Best I've ever seen. They're wonderful!' Granddad yells. 'Where are they coming from?'

Good question. I look around to ask Reggie. He's gone. I peer into the darkness. I can just see him crouching by the light of the fire. I half expect him to be lighting the fireworks. Funny thing is he doesn't seem to be doing anything. I mean, he's just staring into the sky too. Maybe he ran around lighting them all before, so that they went off one after another. It's the only explanation I can think of.

I go across. Just as I reach him, a Roman candle whooshes fireballs of colour. Fills the darkness with globes of fire. It's beautiful. I've never seen anything like it.

'Blimey, these are brilliant! Where d'you get 'em from?'

He looks at me. He's got this puzzled look on his face.

'I didn't. They're k-kind of just here.'

'What d'you mean, "kind of just here"?'

He shrugs. Reggie's good at shrugging. He could give lessons in shrugging. But he's not getting away with it that easily. I can see he doesn't want me to ask questions, so I do.

'Come on, Reggie. What d'you mean? Fireworks don't suddenly turn up for the night like they've got nothing else to do.'

From behind us a rocket fires into the sky.

'L-look at that one.'

'Never mind about that. Where did they come from?'

'Does it m-matter?'

'You didn't nick them, did you?'

All around us rockets fizz, spit, then take off. Storm up in the sky. Die in the night. Then burst into life again. In the corner of the darkness, a fold of shadows, a Catherine wheel spins light. A spiral of colour, spitting golden sparks, like it's telling its own story to the night. It goes on for ages, singing out its life, then stutters to a dying finish. When I look round, there are lots of people over by the bonfire. More are coming over from the next street.

'There's N-Norman and the others.'

'Well, I don't know how you got them, but they're brilliant. I couldn't have imagined fireworks like this, not in my wildest dreams.'

Reggie turns. Gives me a funny look. 'I think you c-could, Alice.' And he says the 'you' in a strange kind of way. Like if it was in a book, it'd be underlined. I think he's got a screw loose.

Norman shouts something about Germans invading and to get our ammunition, or some such rubbish. He takes careful aim at the launching rockets. Shoots with deadly accuracy as they explode.

George and Veronica arrive. Veronica dances around. Centre of attention, as usual. George stands, hands in pockets. Then Veronica comes over.

'Great fireworks. We could see them from the Spicers' bonfire. Much better than theirs.'

Firework after firework lights up the sky, till it seems like it's going to go on for ever. Everybody's saying what a great display it is. I remember I've still got the sparklers in my pocket. I light them from the bonfire and give them to some little kids. They run through the darkness, trailing sparks. Wheeling and turning, making Spitfire noises.

Flash joins in: chasing sparks, chasing his tail, eating smoke, barking. A lot of dogs don't like fireworks, but to Flash it's a big adventure. Mum's right, he is a bit scatty; in a nice way. I reckon his idea of heaven would be riding in the cart with a bone, waving sparklers. You get the feeling if you gave him a lighted sparkler he would run around with it making Spitfire noises too.

One thing's for sure. It's the best bonfire night I could ever have imagined.

Mum gets me up early. We're out of bread. It's cold. I feel sleepy still, only half awake. Snow has scattered itself, icing-sugar white, on the pavements. I carefully tread the first shapes. Announce myself in footprints to the morning. Breathe whispers of secret fog to heaven.

The snow changes the streets. Deadens noise. Footsteps become a crunch of tight sound. I put out my arm and let some flakes settle on it, fragile papery layers of light, crystal-thin. I catch some on my tongue; they melt like dreams.

I'm cold. My shoe has a hole in it. The snow soaks my sock, freezing my foot. I move quickly, half walking, half sliding on the pavements. I have to cross the old bomb site where we had our bonfire last night; the ashes are still smouldering. I stand looking around for a while. Remembering. Trying to see the colour of last night in the silver-white snow sky of the day. I mimic the noises of rockets, pirouette like the Catherine wheel. Get embarrassed. Hope no one's seen me.

I make my way down to the street, slipping and sliding, to where the Spicer twins were last night. Then I take a short cut across another lot of rubble. As I cross I can see where they had their bonfire. Smouldering ashes are still sending wispy signals. Doesn't look as though it was as big as ours.

I pull out a dead rocket case from the snow. I find a banger case. Score a goal with it. Scoop up a handful of Roman candle shells, blackened and charred, throw them into the air as if I could toss life back into them. They fall limply back to earth. I squint at the scorched instructions on a big rocket: *Light the blue touchpaper, then stand well back . . .*

I remember I'm supposed to be buying bread, cross the road to the shop, still thinking about our bonfire and theirs. But I've got this feeling that something's not right. What is it?

I stop, as if the empty street has just called out my name, and stand there for a while holding the rocket case in my hand, thinking about it. I try to think clearly. *Be logical, Alice. Work it out.* I need someone to talk to.

'You there, Sherlock?'

'As ever, dear girl.'

'Think we've got another mystery on our hands.'

'I'm your man, then.'

'Something's not right here.'

'Such as?'

'Something's missing.'

'What is, dear girl?'

'I'm not sure.'

Sherlock sucks at his pipe. 'Well, if it's any help, the first thing I always did was to look for the evidence.'

That's it! Evidence. Or rather, no evidence. I solve the puzzle. Except the puzzle becomes a riddle. The answer becomes a question.

I know what's missing, but it doesn't make sense. You can't make nonsense make sense.

I turn and run back to the old bomb site as fast as I can. Bert will be furious if I'm late with the bread, but I have to know.

I run the whole way. I pass Norman. He stops to talk. I don't. Calls out after me. 'Brilliant fireworks last night, Al. My dad said they must have cost a fortune.'

I get to the site of our bonfire and stand there, sucking in cold air, hands on hips. I get my breath back. The snow is getting thicker now, the powdery white coating is already nearly an inch thick. My heart is pounding. I start looking for clues, keeping to the edge of the bomb site first, and working my way around. I hope I'm going to find what I'm looking for. If I don't, I won't know what to think.

I search for over half an hour. Carefully, eyes on the ground, I cover the whole area, but they're not there. No sign. In my head, more questions. There must be answers, there've got to be. But there aren't.

# ★★★ 9 Missing evidence

I walk slowly home. I try to think. Where the Spicers had their bonfire, the ground is littered with dead cases – everywhere you look you can see burned-out firework shells. But where we had the biggest and best fireworks that anyone had ever seen there isn't a single firework case to be found. Not one. That's what was missing. It's as if our fireworks never existed.

I'm still trying to puzzle it out as I walk down the passage. I go down to the front room. Open the door.

He's sitting at the table, his fingers drumming on the top. He looks up.

'Where you been?'

'Getting the bread.'

His eyes narrow. 'Don't lie to me.'

'I'm not lying.'

'Well, where is it then?'

The bread. Blow and bugger.

'I forgot it.'

He stands up and moves towards me. 'Liar. You were with that boy again.'

'I wasn't! Ask Mum.'

'I don't need to ask anyone anything. Get to your room and stay there!'

'But I just . . . '

He turns to me. His eyes fix me, like they're boring through my skin. My words die.

'I know you were with that boy last night.'

There's something in his voice. Like a threat. Like his voice is acid eating into everything. I take a step back.

'I – I was with a lot of people.'

His eyes are still fixed on me in that cold stare. Like he knows.

'Don't back chat. I told you to keep away from him. He's trouble. D'you hear me?'

I don't say anything. I want to argue, but I'm afraid.

'I said, do you hear me?' His voice sinks, sounds threatening. My cheek burns.

'I hear you.'

I go out through the kitchen. Mumble under my breath as I walk up the passage. I open the door to the bedroom. Don't go in. Slam it hard. Wait in the shadows for a while in case he comes to check on me. He doesn't. I wait. I wait a little longer than usual. When Bert's like that he scares me. Still, it's all quiet now so I'll just nip up to Reggie's for a sec and tell him about the firework cases. See what he makes of it.

The stairs are dark, as usual. The bare bulb at the very top blinks out just enough light for a flea's tea party. I take another look. Make sure Bert's not watching me from somewhere. There are lots of creepy shadows about in this old passage but I can't see him. So, here goes.

Slowly I start to creep up the first stairs. Glad to get away. These first treads are the noisy ones so I have to watch it here. I take a couple at a time. Not jumping. Just long strides, then carefully haul myself up by the banisters. I'm lost in my thoughts so I don't notice at first. Then I do. These stairs always creak. But for some reason they're not creaking now. They seem sort of soft. Soft? They've never been soft before. It's like walking on mud.

I look down at my feet but it's so dark I can't see a thing. Something's wrong. I know it. I can feel it. Trouble is, I don't know what. It smells different too. Not the usual hundred-year-old-armpit smell but a kind of earth smell. Like trees and plants and stuff. Like I've stumbled into a jungle. Jungle? Get a grip, Alice, you're losing it. What was that? A noise. Sounded like a bird singing. Can't be. Right. The quicker I get up to Reggie's flat the better.

I try to move faster, but it's difficult. I'm just about to turn on to the first landing when I trip over something. Go sprawling headfirst into the dark. Must just be some old rubbish someone's chucked down. I could have broken my neck.

I reach out and try to feel what it is. Yuk! It's slimy . . . thick . . . feels a bit like . . . wood . . . a branch of some kind and there's . . . leaves! It's got leaves on it. Can't be. I hold it up. It's like some sort of creeper. I try to move it but it's too heavy. I can't budge it. I go to step back and nearly fall over another one. They seem to be everywhere. And the ground is shifting under my feet. Turning to mud. A swamp. There are insects buzzing around my head. The creaking stairs have become a pathway through a jungle.

I walk through a curtain of creepers. This is just like one of the games I play. I'm an explorer coming through an equatorial jungle. In the jungle game I get trapped, caught up in giant creepers, but I'm not playing any games now. What is this, what's going on?

I feel something slip around my ankle, then up my leg. It's rough. Cuts into my flesh. I bend down. Grab it. It's one of the creepers. It tightens. Ouch! That hurts. I try to pull it off. Another comes from nowhere and curls over my hand. The banisters are changing from solid wooden rails to twisting, slithering creepers. It's like the shadows on the stairs are all coming to life. They reach out to me: curling tentacles twisting around my arms, grabbing at my body.

I pull hard. I have to try to get out of this. I can feel more and more of them, like wriggling fat snakes. I try really hard not to get frightened but my heart is bumping like a dodgem car. My feet are sinking in the swamp. I need help.

Although I don't have a real dad, sometimes I get a funny feeling that someone is there. Like when I'm in trouble. No one flies down to my rescue like Superman; I'm not saying that, it's just a tiny feeling. That feather-brushing-my-face feeling. It happens now and I get an idea from out the blue.

Mrs Cassidy! Of course. Her door is just round the

corner. If only I could move. Trouble is, I can't. There are creepers all around me now. They're coming out of the walls. Up through the floor. Writhing up my legs. Tying themselves in knots around me.

I start to panic. I'm thrashing around but I can't break away. I take in a deep breath and scream as loud as I've ever done in my life. It explodes into the air. Rings around the empty staircase, bounces back off the cold stone walls.

'Who is it? Who's there?'

Mrs Cassidy's door swings open. Light floods out. Soundlessly the creepers slide out of sight. Slink back into the walls and floors. Dissolve. Disappear. The banisters grow firm, the ground is solid under my feet. It's like the jungle world has collapsed in on itself. A tangle of thoughts has dissolved.

Mrs Cassidy's head peeps around the door.

'Who is it? What's going on out there?'

I feel a bit sheepish.

'Hello, Mrs Cassidy. It's only me.'

'Alice? Is that you? Where are you?'

'Down here, Mrs Cassidy.'

'What you doing, love? You all right?'

'Not really, Mrs Cassidy. I was trapped in a jungle by some creepers and I couldn't get out. Sorry I screamed so loud.'

'Terrible places them jungles, Alice. My Fred was in one during the war, you know. Bit early for games though, love.'

'It wasn't a game.'

'If you say so, dear. We're just having our breakfast. Nice bowl of porridge with a bit of syrup. Or, in my Fred's case, a nice bowl of syrup with a bit of porridge. Sweet tooth you know, ducks. You all right now?'

'Think so.'

'Too many comics, I expect. Them stairs are dark. Bit scary. Smells like a jungle an' all, sometimes.'

'Seemed real to me.'

'My Fred reckons you've got a vivid imagination, Alice. "Betty," he says, "that young Alice has got a vivid imagination." Know what that is, dear?'

'Not really.'

'Means colourful.'

'Right.'

I'm not sure if she thinks that's good or bad.

'I'd best get on, Mrs Cassidy.'

I start to go back down the stairs.

She shakes her head, mutters,'I don't know, jungle indeed.'

Shuts her door. The light goes.

I'm still feeling a bit shaky. One thing being in a game when you know you're in one. Another being in one when you don't. I'll go and see Reggie later. Think I've had enough excitement for one day.

I'm almost down when I see him. He hasn't seen me yet. He's in the shadow at the bottom of the stairs. Our front room door is open and a wedge of light escapes. It catches part of his face. He's leaning against the wall smoking, staring up.

I stop. Crouch in the darkness, watching him. He's got this twisted smile on his face. Like he knows what's happened. But that's impossible. Maybe he heard me scream.

He takes one last puff, then flicks his cigarette into the air. He always does that. Sparks fly off. He turns, goes back into the front room.

## ★★★ 10 Lolly sticks and the law of averages

Bonfire night becomes another memory. Locked away. I try to stop thinking about the weird things that have been going on. Strange things happen sometimes. Especially in dark places when shadows come out to play.

Christmas comes. Reggie and Granddad go away somewhere. I've never known anybody round here ever go away. Except some of the older boys – to prison.

I've decided not to play games on the stairs any more. I'm letting my imagination get the better of me. My mum says that. 'You mustn't let your imagination get the better of you, sweetheart.' Sounds like I'm in a fight with my own imagination. Alice Makin in the blue corner; her imagination in the red. Will it get the better of her in tonight's big fight? Ding, ding, round one. Come out boxing.

When we get back to school after the holidays Reggie's not there. I wonder if he's going to come back at all. But after a couple of weeks he turns up. Funny, it's as if he's never been away. Our friendship's a favourite old jumper.

You might not wear it for a while, but when you put it back on it's just as comfortable as when you last wore it. And you know you're still going to be wearing it when all the other jumpers, the ones you thought you'd wear for ever, you don't like any more.

I never did get a chance to ask Reggie about the fireworks. I suppose he must have found them. That's what he must have meant when he said they were 'kind of just there'. Or maybe he did pinch them. You never know. But not being able to find any leftover cases was really strange. Most likely the wind blew them away.

Anyway, I've been too busy to think about that. We've got some good news. Mum is going to have a baby. And I'm really busy at school: Sister Bernadette has asked me to write a play. She wants our form to put it on at the end of the summer term, for the junior school down the road. It seemed a bit of a scary idea at first. I wasn't sure I could do it. But then I had this great idea: I'd try to write a play about Sherlock Holmes and Doctor Watson and how they get called in to investigate a mystery in Nursery Rhyme land.

I told some of the others and George Morgan asked if he could be Sherlock Holmes. I think he thinks Holmes is like one of the detectives in the comic books he reads and he'll get a gun. Then Veronica found out George was going to be in it and suddenly decided she just had to play Watson. Interesting. She's good, though. I told Mum. She said, 'I'm not surprised, she's a proper little actress, that one,' in that funny kind of way she has when she's saying one thing, but really means something different.

I've known Veronica Silk and George since we were in the Infants together at Saint Mary's. George used to sit behind me. One day while we were doing Art, I heard this snip and felt a tug at my hair. He'd cut a lump of it off. Veronica said he did it because he liked me. It made me wonder what he would do if he *didn't* like someone. But he's all right really. I wanted him and Reggie to be friends. George tried, but Reggie didn't. He wasn't rude or anything, just . . . well, distant, I suppose.

I sometimes feel Reggie's got something he really wants to say to me. To get off his chest. And everyone else is just getting in the way. I asked him about it once. He just shrugged.

And so the months go by. Winter snow melts. Time warms its hands by the light of the morning. In school we daydream through lessons, play street games in alleys, hide and seek times, sing songs without names, with words without end. Run in and out of days, make friends with a smile, enemies with a look.

'Alice, you in there?'

I'm working on the play in the old air-raid shelter when I hear Reggie scrambling across the bomb site. We usually prop a bit of wood over the opening to the shelter, but it's such a nice day I didn't bother. It's nice and light in here, what with the big holes in the canvas roof.

At first I don't answer. Once I start on a story I can't get the characters out of my head and I'm always thinking about what's going to happen to them.

'Alice?'

'Yeah, I'm here.'

Flash barks at the sound of my voice. They both appear at the opening. 'What you d-doing?'

'I'm writing the play for school.'

Flash pushes in like he owns the place. Sniffs around. Sees an old piece of paper on the floor. Pushes it with his nose. Looks for a minute like he's trying to read it. Then changes his mind and starts growling at it.

Reggie ducks in. Sits down. Looks over my shoulder, which I hate.

'W-what's it about?'

'Sherlock Holmes. He's this—'

'I know. Famous d-detective. I like him too. I know all his adventures.'

'Well, you don't know this one, 'cos I'm making it up.'

'Want to go over the p-park?'

'No, I think I'll stay and do my play. I'm getting into it now.'

'Come on, it's n-nice out.'

'No. I wanna get this done.'

'Come on, you can tell m-me all about the play on the way. I've got some money. I'll buy you an ice lolly if you like.'

'That's bribery.'

'So?'

Oh well, we've all got our weaknesses. I put my stuff away in my biscuit tin. Touch the girl on the swing for good luck. I've made a little secret space where I hide it. You never know when the Spicers are going to come snooping around.

Outside the sun is showing off, splashing warm on the streets. I'm glad spring is here, it's my favourite time of the year. It's like everything is waking up again, getting ready for a new start. There are still puddles left over from yesterday's rain.

We stop to make mud balls. Throw them at the side of a building. Flash runs after them like he's some great retriever dog, leaps into the air barking. Some of the mud balls stick, some splatter into goo and slide slowly down the wall in disgustingly beautiful patterns. It's really babyish, but that's the kind of thing we do. Best thing is, we don't care.

I tell Reggie about my play as we leave Hawkins Street, turn right into Sidney Street, over Mile End Road, and head for Vicky Park. Reggie's got Flash on a piece of string because of the traffic. Flash likes string, but not when it's tied to his collar. Every now and then he stops and tries to pull it off.

The walk is long and warm. We cross Mile End Road to Mr Giovanni's sweet shop, stop for a rest and admire the view. In the window, alongside the sleeping tabby cat, colours clash and riot in sweet jars – row upon row of them, marching into the distance – liquorice curls, aniseed twists, saucers fly, powered by sherbet. The smell of cough candy beckons us with a sly finger. Winter warmers wait to heat tongues.

We go in. Mr Giovanni is Italian, and sing-songs his words as if they were poetry. His face is a gob-stopper, multi-coloured. His chins are jellies. He makes the best ice cream in the world. And his own drinks and ice lollies. One bottle keeps you going all day. You can burp for ever on his raspberryade. It bubbles on your tongue and cascades into flavour down your throat.

Some time ago he came up with a new idea. When he makes a batch of ice lollies he writes a number on one of the sticks. You can't see it until you've eaten the lolly, because it's covered by the ice. If you get the stick with the number on it you can exchange it for a prize – anything you want in the whole shop!

'If I ever w-win I'd have that jar of cough candy.'

'Why? You ain't got a cough.'

'Or a jar of those p-pineapple cubes.'

'If I ever win, I'll have the box of chocolates in the window.'

The box has a yellow ribbon around it, tied in a big bow.

On the lid is a picture. I love this picture – it's an old thatched cottage in a country lane. It's summer, the windows of the cottage have beautiful little squared panes of glass in them, and the sun, bright as a newly minted penny, winks back its light from the windows. The front garden is full of flowers. There's a washing line flying kites of clothes, and you can just see the back garden with its apple trees. A white horse is nuzzling the grass in the field behind. Outside the front door a woman in a bright summer dress sits in a rocking chair.

'Come on, l-let's get a lolly. You never know your luck.'

'I know mine – bad.'

'You ever w-won anything?'

'No, never. I wish just for once I could. It's my mum's birthday on Wednesday. I'd give anything to win that box of chocolates for her.'

'Law of averages s-says you'll w-win something one day.'

'Do the ice lollies know that, though?'

'Maybe we'll buy two. Law of averages says two chances are better than one.'

The ice lollies are refreshing. Like your tongue's been dropped into a bath of freezing fruity water. I break a bit of mine off and give it to Flash. He wolfs it down, except for a little bit that gets stuck on his nose. He tries to lick it off. It melts into a red moustache.

Once we get outside, it's not far to go to the park. I'm looking forward to seeing the swans on the boating lake. They're so graceful – one long curve really, a gliding question mark. The sun sucks at my lolly, dribbles juice down my hand. Reggie bought a bottle of lemonade, too.

'Want a s-swig?'

'Please. Can you hold my lolly?'

We pass them backwards and forwards. It's a rule that you can't take a bite from someone else's lolly while you're holding it for them.

I take a gulp of the lemonade.

'Oi, th-that's enough.'

'Hold on. I only had a sip.'

He pulls it away too quickly and some of the drink goes up my nose. I burp.

'Oi, d-don't do that.'

I get the giggles. I always do when I burp.

'Alice, s-stop doing that.'

'I can't!'

I get caught between coughing, burping and laughing. It starts Reggie off. When he sees me laughing, he always starts too.

I finish the lolly before the sun has a chance to do it for me. As we pass a bin he throws in the bottle and holds out his hand for my stick. I suck off the last bit of ice and give the stick to him. He goes to drop it in the bin.

I wish I'd won. I imagine it. In my head I see the numbers appearing on the stick. It's so real I can see it. We're waiting to cross the road.

'Cor, l-look at that.'

I think he's seen something across the road.

'What?'

'Your lolly stick.' He holds it like a conjuror about to do a trick. I try to see it in his hand.

'What about it?'

'Can't you s-see?'

'See what?'

'Look at the t-top.'

'I will if you take your hand out the way.'

'You're never g-going to believe it.'

'Believe what?'

Suddenly, he pulls his hand away. The conjuror pulling out the rabbit.

'You've d-done it!'

'Pack it in, Reggie. Done what?'

'It's the l-lucky number.'

'Don't muck around, Reggie. That's not funny.'

'I'm not. See for yourself.'

He shoves the lolly stick at me. There, in bold black writing, is the number twenty-seven. I can't believe it. I must have bought hundreds of lollies in that shop, but never the lucky one.

'Blimey . . . I've won. I've won something at last!'

I grab him and plant a kiss on his cheek. He goes red.

'I didn't see the number. How did I miss that?'

Part of my brain dances with joy. I've got the lucky stick. I can get the chocolates for Mum. The other part is whirring, telling me that something funny is going on here. There was no number on that stick when I gave it to Reggie.

# ★★★ 11 Picksmeup and dropsy

We carry on to the park. No sense in walking around with a box of chocolates. We'd probably eat them all. We can get them on the way back.

Just inside the park is a fenced-off area like a playground with a few play things in it. Really they're for little kids. They're mostly old and beat up. Three swings with shiny, worn wooden seats. A big wooden roundabout with chipped green metal holding-on bits. An umbrella that no matter how hard you push when you jump on it still limps around lopsidedly like a one-legged tortoise. And one of those long metal rocking things that have a horse's head at one end and something that's supposed to look like a tail at the other end. There are little metal seats which you're supposed to sit on, although when we were little kids we used to stand up on the running boards and work up really hard so that the whole thing jerked up and down like a rodeo horse. It's better if you sit at the horse's head and hold on to the neck. Then you get thrown all over the place.

As I look across I see a familiar figure. Norman comes

here a lot. Like I said, it's supposed to be for younger kids but he doesn't care. He's sitting on one of the swings. I wave. He waves back. He looks lonely. I turn to Reggie.

'I'm just going over to see Norman for a minute.'

'All right. I'll go and s-see if I can find Charlie. I'll be at the lake when you're ready.'

I cross the little road that runs through Vicky Park and go into the playground.

'Hello, Norm.'

He smiles. 'Wotcha, Al.'

'What you doing?'

'Swinging.'

'I can see that. I mean, what you doing here on your own?'

'Nothing, just thinking.'

'You've got all blood on your knee, Norm.'

'Yeah, I know.'

'How d'you do it?'

'I fell off the swing. I'm always doing that.'

His arms are cradled around the metal chains that hold the seat, so that he's more rocking on the seat than he is swinging. I'm about to ease myself on to the one next to him.

'Hold on.'

He reaches across and wipes the seat with the sleeve of his jacket.

I get on. Start to swing slowly.

'So, what you thinking about?'

'I saw you and Reggie coming into the park and I was thinking I wished I was you.'

'Don't think you'd fit into my dresses.'

'No, I mean I wish I was clever like you.'

'I'm not clever, Norm.'

You are.'

'Why d'you say that?'

He thinks for a while. Starts to swing slowly.

'Well, when you make things up all the teachers and everybody say nice things about you; what a good imagination you've got, and that. When I do it they just shout at me and tell me off.'

I'm still rocking. The thing with Norman is that it sometimes takes a while to work out where he's going. Sherlock would do it by subtle questioning. Craftily deducing what was going on in Norman's head by logic.

'How d'you mean?'

As he's swinging he lets one foot trail in the dirt, scuffing the toes of his shoes. Good job my mum isn't here.

'Like the other day in class. You made up a story and got a prize. But when I made one up I got told it was a lie and a venial sin and sent to Sister and had to miss play.'

First piece of evidence. I have to be careful how I handle this. Mustn't disturb the scene of the crime. Leave my prints all over Norman's feelings.

'Was your story the one you told Mr O'Cain? About your dad being a secret service agent working for MI5?'

He scuffs some more.

'Yeah. That was it.'

'Thing is, your dad's a milkman, Norm, and he delivers milk to Watney Street, which is where Mr O'Cain lives.'

'So?'

'So, Mr O'Cain knows he's a milkman, not a secret service agent.'

Norman pushes off, keeps pace with me.

'Maybe my dad's undercover and he's really going round tracking down escaped German prisoners of war and poisoning them with milk.'

I start to swing higher. Lean backwards. Lean forwards. Backwards. Forwards.

'Never thought of that, Norm.'

The wind wakes up. Who's for a joy-ride? Buzzes around my ears. Faster, Alice. Faster. Forwards and back. Higher and higher. I lose my stomach. Find it. Norman starts to work up too. But we're not together. He's up. I'm down. I call across as we pass, 'Tell you one thing.'

He calls back; I can tell by the way his voice wavers that he's losing his stomach too.

'What's that?'

'It's a good story.'

He smiles.

'Thanks, Al.'

'Better than some of mine.'

'Al?'

'What?'

'D'you reckon if we went too high we'd go right around

the top bar and get wrapped up in the chains?'

'Dunno. Want to try?'

'No, I get sick if I go too high.'

'What if you have to parachute out of an aeroplane when you join the army?'

'I'd just pull me balaclava up so I couldn't see.'

'Fair enough. Look, I've got to go now, Norm. Reggie'll be waiting for me.'

'Here, Al?'

'What?'

I'm starting to slow down. It feels nice. Not leaning back or forward. Just sitting. The wind slows to a lullaby.

'D'you reckon Mr O'Cain might be an escaped German prisoner of war?'

Norman's still swinging too. We're in tandem now.

'Don't think many Germans would be called Mr O'Cain, Norm.'

'Why?'

'It's Irish.'

'Is that why he talks funny?'

'It's called an accent, Norm.'

My swing stops. Norman stops his by scuffing his shoes in the dirt. I get off. I get the feeling he doesn't want me to go.

'Want a quick game of picksmeup and dropsy?'

We used to play picksmeup when we were little kids. I haven't played it for years.

'Long as it's quick.'

I go over to the old roundabout and start pushing. It's big and heavy but once it gets going it soon picks up speed. Norman looks for a small stick. Old lolly sticks are best. He joins me. Helps push.

'Ready?'

'Few more pushes; let's get it going really fast.'

The roundabout comes to life, whizzes round, blurring the world against the background of the trees.

'Go.'

We both jump on. Me on one side, Norman on the other. Crouch into a sitting position on the running board. It's not easy to hear, what with the wind whistling and the roundabout creaking. Norman calls out, 'Dropsy.'

Somewhere out of my sight, he drops the stick on to the ground. Next he jumps off and runs around clinging on to the roundabout and pushing as if his life depended on it, while counting to ten. As the roundabout spins around at breakneck speed I have to spot where the stick is, lean out and pick it up before he gets to ten. You have to be really careful. If you lose your grip you can get shot off and end up with a sore backside.

He's pushing fast. I look for the stick, see it near some leaves, but before I can get my fingers to it I flash past. The roundabout whizzes. Five-six-seven. I've spun back to where the stick is. I reach out. Eight-nine. Grab it. Shout out, 'Picksmeup. One-nil lead.'

Norman jumps on the running board. Crouches. I drop the stick.

'Dropsy.'

I jump off. Start pushing as hard as I can and start counting.

'Here, Al.'

'What?'

'Know what you were saying?'

'About what?'

He gets the stick too quickly. 'Picksmeup-dropsy.'

He jumps off. I jump on.

'My story.'

'Hold on, not so fast. What about it?'

'You said it was a good story. Mr O'Cain said it was a bunch of lies.'

I see the stick, pick it up.

'Picksmeup. Ouch.'

'You all right?'

'Scraped me fingers. Dropsy. So what about it?'

I jump off. He jumps on.

'Thing is, you're clever so you know the difference. But how do I know if I'm just telling lies or making up a good story? You sure you dropped the stick, I can't see . . . hold on . . . picksmeup!'

'Good question, Norm. My stepdad doesn't think I know the difference either.'

Norman stands up on the running board. Sits on the top bit of the roundabout, stick in hand.

'So what's a good answer?'

The roundabout slows.

'Think you have to work that out for yourself, Norm.'

'Al?'

'Yeah?'

'I feel a bit sick.'

'Yeah, know what you mean.'

''Ere, Al?'

'Yes, Norm?'

'D'you think I could ever write a play like what you do?'

''Course you could; it's easy.'

'How easy?'

I look back at the swings moving gently in the breeze. Look at the blood drying on his knee.

'Easy as falling off a swing, Norm.'

He pulls his balaclava down under his chin and smiles.

## ★★★ 12 Getting wet

Reggie's sitting on the end of the little wooden jetty by the boating pond. Flash is looking at his reflection in the water. Tries to dip his paws in.

'You t-took your time.'

'I was talking to Norman.'

On the jetty, red-faced men fish. They tie worms to hooks, talking about all the big fish they caught last week when there was no one there to see them. I look around for Charlie. He's painting an old, upturned rowing boat. He smiles when he sees us. He's a walking plant – flower-pot boots, a grizzled beard of white prickles. We help him to look after his customers sometimes: take money, help them into the boats.

'Charlie s-said he wasn't very busy; we can take one out for a while.'

'Bags you row.'

'I b-bags you row.'

'I said it first.'

'I said it s-second.'

Charlie looks up. 'Leave Flash here, I'll look after him. Looks like he's in need of a bowl of water.'

Flash doesn't seem to like that idea; tries to get into the boat. Charlie goes to grab him. Flash ducks between his legs. Reggie calls him, makes him sit. Flash doesn't look too pleased about that either. I think he fancied doing a bit of rowing himself.

We step into the boat. I take one oar, Reggie takes the other. We work well together and soon get halfway across the lake, heading for Swan Island. The sky is clear and blue. We stop rowing and rest. It's great out here, like being miles away from everybody. The people on the jetty have shrunk to doll size.

We drift around the other side of Swan Island. I sit back. Overhead, birds swoop, darting their black, cut-out shapes against the sun. The air is calm, tranquil. I trail my fingers through the water – cool and dark and deep. The sun is hot on my head. I close my eyes, lift my face up. Once, people used to worship the sun. I can see why. I decide I'm just going to think of nice things. Thatched cottages, the chocolates I'm going to get for Mum, and let my mind drift off. The boat is a cradle. It's so peaceful here. The light on the water. The sound of the birds. I feel the world rocking me to sleep.

Something changes. I open my eyes. The sun is fading. Clouds have appeared from nowhere. They're bubbling in the sky. Simmering. The little boat jerks. The clouds boil. The sky is changing colour. The surface of the water rises and falls. I sit up and look around, wondering what's going on. Everything seems restless, disturbed, like some sea monster is trying to surface below us. I look up at the sun again. It seems to be shrinking, collapsing into itself. The light deserts the sky. A strange yellow mist rises up.

I look at Reggie. He's staring out at the water, looking puzzled.

'What's going on?'

He shrugs. 'D-don't know. It's scary though.'

Rain starts falling. Heavy, dense rain. The little boat's a toy now: feather light, getting thrown around. It pitches and tosses. It's getting darker. It's the middle of the day, but I can only just see Reggie.

I hear my voice. It sounds frightened. 'Come on, we'd better get back.'

I put my oar into the water, pull on it hard. He doesn't move. 'Come *on*, Reggie!'

The rain's heavier now. It's like someone has turned the sky upside down, and all the rain up there has come down at once. It drives into our faces. My clothes are soaked already. I wonder if we can make it to Swan Island. Get some shelter there. Reggie's still staring back towards the jetty, water running from his hair.

'Reggie, will you start rowing? I can't do it all by—'

Then I see what he's looking at. It's like a punch in the face from your best friend. Unexpected. Coming towards us from the jetty, a roll of water is moving across the surface of the lake. Heading in our direction. High as a bus. Tumbling, somersaulting water.

'What is that?'

The rain has soaked both of us. It's streaming from Reggie's hair and running down his face. He squints to see.

'I d-don't know for sure, but . . .' He puts his hand to his forehead to keep the rain from his eyes. 'It looks like a t-tidal wave.'

'A what?'

The wall of water gets higher with every second. Roaring like a waterfall. Rolling like a train. Sucking up water. Getting bigger. Wider. Faster. It fills the horizon. Hisses milk-white foam.

'It's w-what you g-get in the s-sea.'

'But this is a lake.'

'I kn-know.'

'If that hits us, the boat's gonna be crushed into matchwood!'

I can't believe that two minutes ago we were sitting in the sun. Now we can't even see Swan Island. We can't see anything. We can hear, though. Hear the roar of the wave as it thunders towards us like an earthquake, pushing before it a wall of deafening, ear-splitting sound. The boat is uncontrollable, doing its best to shake us out.

'Start rowing!' I scream, as loudly as I can. 'We've gotta get away!'

Reggie picks up his oar. We try to row in time. The water is as heavy as lead. We're rowing through concrete.

'It's c-coming in.'

I look down. The bottom of the boat is filling with water. 'We're gonna sink! Pull harder.'

My hands are already sore. Skin rubbing off on the rough oars.

'Keep together!'

'I'm d-doing my best.'

I pull as hard as I can. I can barely see Reggie now. I can just hear his voice above the noise. I'm starting to panic when a picture comes into my mind. Like someone's painting it there. It's a weird feeling. Takes a while to see what it is. Then I do. Swan Island. Of course. That's it.

I call out, 'Let's try to get to the island. We can shelter there.'

'What?'

'I said – never mind, just keep rowing.'

Reggie tries to change position, but as he does he knocks the oars into the water. I want to shout and scream at him. I don't. If I'm going to die, I'd rather die thinking about being in the shelter of Swan Island. I feel panicky. My thoughts cartwheel. Then suddenly the boat moves – on its own. We're not rowing. It just starts to move, heading for Swan Island, for cover. This is mad.

I try to look at Reggie, but can't see his face at all now. How's he doing it – making the boat go without oars? But I don't care as long as we get there. We make it. The wind starts to drop. I'm just about to breathe a sigh of relief when I look up. The wave is coming again, sweeping in a long, high bend round the edge of Swan Island, almost as if it's looking for us. It's higher and faster. This time it's really going to swamp us, make matchwood of the boat and drag us down to the bottom of the lake. I'm soaking. My teeth are chattering.

I wonder what it's going to be like when it hits us. Don't have to wonder for long. I peer through my fingers. It's on us, filling the sky. It seems to freeze for a moment in mid-air, towering above us. Then I get that feather feeling again. Light as a raindrop. A bead of dew. Mad. But I know what I have to do. I screw up my eyes. Concentrate my mind like a magnifying glass focusing the sun on paper, waiting for it to burst into flames. I'm seeing a picture of us sitting in the sun again under a quiet, blue sky. Warm and safe.

# ★★★ 13 Challenges

Time melts.

The sun pops into the sky. Instant warmth spreads through my body. The sky fills up with blue, birds glide over the still, calm water, looping in search of lunch. As suddenly as the storm came, it's gone.

I say, 'What the . . . ?'

And stop.

I can't believe what's happened. We're both still alive and bone dry. This is mad! Maybe I drifted off to sleep and dreamed the whole thing. I look at Reggie. I see something in his eyes, and know it wasn't a dream. He just looks puzzled. Whereas I'm scared out of my wits. I can feel my hands shaking. If it happened once, it can happen again, and I'm not sticking around to find out if it's going to. The oars drift by; I reach out and grab them.

'Come on, let's get going'

I start to row by myself. Pull as hard as I can. Cut through the calm, still water. Keep looking behind. It seems to take ages to get back. Sweat streams down my shoulders.

On the jetty everything is normal. The same fishermen

are laughing and chatting. No sign of a tidal wave. No one has been washed away. There isn't a puddle in sight. We hit the jetty hard.

'Oi, careful . . . '

Charlie is still painting the upturned boat. Looks up.

'Oh, it's you two. You were quick. What happened, see the Loch Ness monster?'

I have to get out. I'm scared that if I look around that wall of water will be right behind. I get up too quickly. Catch my knees. Skin grazes. Flesh scrapes, blotches red. I've got to get away from here. Slip. One foot goes into the water, but I stumble up on to the jetty.

Charlie holds out a hand. Looks surprised.

'Steady on. You all right, Alice?'

I don't take his hand. Stumble again. Half trying to work out what's just happened, half trying to block it out as impossible. I can't think properly because I'm still too scared. I run up the jetty. Don't know where I'm going. Anywhere away from here.

'Alice, w-wait.'

I hear Reggie's voice through the maze of my thoughts.

'Where are you g-going?'

Don't reply.

'Alice!'

His footsteps pound behind me. Flash comes barking after him. I clear the jetty, dodging fishermen, tripping over their baskets. Angry voices are hurled after me. I reach the grass and throw myself down. It feels warm. Safe.

Smells new-mown. Get my breath back. Reggie arrives. Sprawls next to me.

'Why d-didn't you wait?'

Flash arrives, thinks I want to play, nips at my arms. I push him away.

'What for? Something else to happen?'

I'm still breathing heavily. Words squeeze out.

'That was weird. I don't know about you, but I'm scared. Whatever that was could have killed us. And we were the only ones to see it. It's like none of that was real. Like something was controlling it.'

What he should say is something like, 'I'm scared too, Alice. I'm scared out of my life. You don't get tidal waves on a lake. Boats don't start rowing themselves. What's going on?'

That's what he should have said. That would have made us the same. Together. Trying to sort things out. To unbend the kinks in the unknown, straighten out the mystery, solve it in a single straight line of common sense.

He doesn't. Instead, in a quiet voice, more like he's talking to himself than me, he says, 'I think someone is trying to frighten us.'

I sit with my head between my knees. My heart is slowing. I look up at him. 'Frighten us? What are you talking about?'

But he's not listening. He's staring at something.

'What is it? What are you looking at?'

There's a figure standing at the far side of the lake. Seems to be looking towards us. A man. He's standing in the shade of some trees, so I can't really make him out. Blue smoke coils from the cigarette he's holding in his hand, drifting out of the shadows into the sunshine.

'Just thought I recognized that man. D'you?'

I look again. Hesitate. There's something familiar, but he's too deep in the shade to see properly.

'Not sure. Look, what did you mean about someone trying to frighten us?'

The man steps further back into the trees and he's gone.

Reggie takes off his glasses. Puts the sticking plaster back on properly. He seems to be acting mysteriously. Like he's got a secret that he's not sure about sharing.

'You know something, don't you? You know what happened out there?'

'I don't w-want to say, Alice . . . not yet.'

'Yet? So you do know something!' I shriek at him, my anger a balloon filling fast. 'Look, you, we could have been killed. If you know something, tell me.'

'I c-can't. Not until I'm sure. When I am, I'll t-tell you. I promise.'

I'm still shaking. He knows something, all right, but he's made up his mind not to tell me. When Reggie makes up his mind, you can't unmake it.

I get up. 'Well, I've had enough for one day. I'm going.'

'Hold on, I'll c-come with you.'

'Don't bother.'

I get up. Walk off. He follows. I start to calm down a bit.

I walk to Giovanni's. Reggie's slightly behind like he doesn't want to catch up. Suits me. It's as if suddenly I don't know him. I'm walking with a stranger.

Life's funny. For once, I get what I wished for most in the world, and it's not like I thought it would be. Right now the chocolates don't seem so important after all.

I take the stick to the counter. Reggie stays back.

Mr Giovanni is happy for me. 'I'm-a glad-a you kids won something.'

I give him the stick.

He puts on his glasses and looks carefully at the number.

'That's her all right-a. Lucky twenty-seven. The age of-a my son. Whatcha gonna have, young-a lady?'

I say, 'The chocolates, please, Mr Giovanni.'

My voice sounds flat, like I don't care.

'You like-a those chocolates, eh? They're the best. You gonna enjoy them, eh?'

'Yeah. Thanks.'

He gives me the stick back. 'Keep her as a souvenir, eh? Lucky souvenir.'

I nod and smile.

We walk back. Together, but not. Reggie might just as well be on another planet. We reach Mile End Road. As if he's been thinking about it for a long time, he says, 'Look, I think other things are g-going to start happening.'

'You're doing it again.'

'Doing w-what?'

'Talking in code. What things are going to happen.?'

'Things you w-won't expect.'

'Oh, great. That's really helpful. Now I know.'

I've had enough. If someone's got something to say, they should say it.

'Reggie, you've got to stop this.'

'S-stop what?'

'Talking in riddles.'

'Sorry. I don't m-mean to.'

'Well, you are. So keep your mouth shut until you remember how to talk sense.'

'Sorry.'

'And stop saying sorry!'

Now I feel terrible. It's like we don't know each other. Like we've suddenly found out we don't speak the same language.

He stops. 'There's something I've got to d-do. I'll s-see you later.'

'Not if I see you first.'

He turns and walks off. I don't go straight home. I need time to think. So I do what I always do when I need time to think – go for a walk.

I get home just as it's beginning to get dark. I can hear my mum calling my name as I come round the corner into Hawkins Street. The lights on the lampposts are just coming on, floating on the darkness like balloons.

It's been a long day, and for once I'm ready to go in. I walk down the corridor, my footsteps keeping me company. I feel confused and still a bit scared. Like everyone knows some dark secret except me.

At least I've got something for Mum's birthday. It's the first time I've got her something I really want to give her. Not like that jigsaw puzzle with the pieces missing, or the diamond brooch from the jumble sale.

I go down the passage to the front room, open the door. She's sitting at the table, darning a shirt. She looks tired. Her eyes are red-rimmed. She glances up, smiles, looks back down. I still feel funny, like someone's playing games with me, making up new rules for my life. But I've got to make an effort for Mum. Bert's not home, that's a bonus. I hide the box behind my back. Get closer. Then, when I'm on top of her, I plonk it down. 'Happy birthday, Mum.'

She looks up. At the box. 'What's all this?' At me. 'You all right, love? You look as if you've seen a ghost!'

'Yeah, bit of a funny day, that's all. Got you a birthday present. Chocolates.'

'So I see. Where d'you get 'em?'

'Sweet shop.'

'Well, I didn't think it was the butcher's.'

'I won 'em. Got the lucky number.'

She puts down her darning. 'Goodness.' She grins. 'My favourites and all. What a lovely box. It's beautiful.'

'Can I have the lid?'

''Course you can.'

She reaches over. Kisses me.

'Thanks, darlin'. Let's open 'em.' She lifts the lid carefully. Sees four empty cups. 'Mice have been at 'em, I see.'

'I was hungry.'

She offers me the box.

'There's a list of all the centres here. How posh.'

'Best in the shop.'

'Well, you know what they say. Proof of the pudding's in the eatin'.'

She reads the little booklet with the list of centres like it's a novel. Sucking the names. Chewing pronunciations. 'Hazelnut Praline, I think.'

'What's praline?'

'Don't know, but it sounds good.'

I watch her face as she takes out the chocolate and eats it. 'Mmm. Wonderful. Come on, let's get stuck in.'

Later, I take the lid and go into my part of the bedroom. I pull the curtain. Sit on the bed, my head full of thoughts. I'm so tired my eyes hurt, but I can't sleep, can't stop thinking. I close my eyes and see the dark, swirling waters of the lake. Waves tower. I'm in the water. Freezing. My hands grabbing out. But there's nothing to hold on to but thin air. I fall. Sink into the darkness.

Cold-water morning light splashes through the curtains and on to my face. I get up quickly. A night full of weird dreams: rowing boats, tidal waves, chocolates. I have to get all this sorted out. I need answers.

I look under the bed for the box lid. Can't see it. I push my arm under. Sweep it around. Lots of rubbish. Still can't feel the lid. Try again. Still no luck. Crawl under the bed. No sign. I sit on the floor for a while, trying to think exactly what I did with it. I'm sure I put it under the bed. There's only one explanation – Bert. He's always snooping around. He must have found it.

I don't even have a wash. I just pull on my clothes, pull back the curtain and go into the other part of the room. Mum is already up. He's still in bed, fast asleep. He came in late last night. I was still awake and heard him get into bed, so it can't have been him. Suddenly I feel panicky. Something's not right, not as it should be. Mum left the rest of the chocolates on the kitchen table. I go in quickly. Look everywhere. No sign. Not even an empty paper cup. Something digs into my side. The lolly stick. It's still in my pocket. I take it out, go to put it on the windowsill, then pull open the curtains so there's more light. My mouth is suddenly dry. My brain isn't working. Slowly, I turn the lolly stick over. Then turn it over again. I still can't believe what I'm seeing. Or rather what I'm not seeing.

The stick is blank. There's no sign of any number, not even the trace of a mark.

First, fireworks that don't leave cases; then a tidal wave that appears and disappears like magic; a box of chocolates that vanishes into thin air; and now, a number on an ice lolly stick that was there and now isn't. This is all mad! It's barmy.

I need to talk to Reggie, and fast. But there's something else I need to do first. I don't know why I have to do it, I just do.

I can hear Bert moving. He calls out. I run out of the door. I know I'll get it from him when I get back, but I don't care. I run as fast as I can towards Vicky Park.

I stand panting in front of Giovanni's shop. Looking in the window, I stare at a box of chocolates, the box of chocolates that I won yesterday. It's got the same picture on the lid, the same yellow ribbon. I suppose it could be another one, of course. Perhaps Mr Giovanni has just put another box in.

I peer in through cupped hands, squinting hard. There on the ribbon is the same red mark that was on yesterday's box, just as if someone had spilled red ink on it. It's not another box. It's the same box.

I get this funny feeling, like everything that is supposed to be real isn't real any more. Which is daft, but that's how I feel. I turn. Walk away. A shiver of electricity crackles down my spine.

I walk around the park on my own, trying to think. The day smells new, clean. Mist clings, sleep in the eyes of the morning. On the trees, buds peep. The world is turning its coat inside out. Seasons are changing around me, but I feel like I did when I was walking through the ruins after the bonfire, looking for something that wasn't there: like I'm in a bubble where anything can happen. It's exactly the same feeling. Something going on that you don't understand. But someone does. And I'm going to get to the bottom of this if it's the last thing I do.

# ★★★ 14 Truth and lies

I'm determined. I'm confused. I'm angry. I catch him up in the street. Reggie's walking fast, his head down. Forehead creased in a frown. Flash sniffs the gutters, runs to keep up, wags his tail when he sees me. The sun flicks shadows in and out of doorways.

I'm a steamroller. Reggie's the tarmac. I grab his shoulder. 'Right, come on then, let's have it. What's goin' on?'

He stops; looks for a second as if he doesn't know me.

'I'm not asking you, Reggie, I'm telling you. I want to know. Things are turning upside down around me and I think you know what's doing it. For a start . . . ' I shove the lolly stick at him, ' . . . what d'you know about this?'

He takes the stick. Turns it over in his hand and looks hard at me.

'The n-number's gone. I thought it would be.'

I grab his shoulder again. He stops. Turns. Screws up his eyes, the way he does.

'So? Come on. What's going on here? The fireworks, the tidal wave, the lolly stick – what's happening?'

He takes a deep breath. 'It's not easy to explain . . . ' He stops; looks around like he's searching for inspiration.

'You know when you w-want something so bad you feel like you can taste it? Even *see* it?' He looks at me. Waits for a second. 'Well, I can.'

'Reggie, what you on about? You can *what*?'

'S-see it.'

'See *what*, you idiot?'

'See whatever it is I want to see. I m-mean, really see it. Like it's real. But the really incredible thing is . . . ' He stops again, hesitates, ' . . . I can let other people see what I'm seeing. I've got the p-power to show people what's in my mind. I don't know where it comes from b-but . . . '

That's it. He's lost his marbles.

'Reggie, you feeling all right? That is such a load of . . . '

He gives me one of his looks. Screws up his eyes.

'I call it mind-touching because when I do it it's like I'm reaching out and touching other people's minds. Don't suppose it's got a n-name really.'

'Reggie, I couldn't care less what you call it. I'd call it a load of old rubbish. The only thing that's touched around here is you. Right, the joke's over. If you're not going to tell me what's really going on . . . '

He looks hard at me. 'It's n-no joke.'

'Come on, you're not serious, are you?'

I can see he is.

'I'm just trying to help. You wanted to know what's been happening, and I'm t-telling you.'

'All right, then. Just let's say that for a minute I believe you – which I don't – are you really trying to tell me that the fireworks, the chocolates, the lolly, all that stuff happened because you're making what you imagine real? Like making a dream come true? You're trying to tell me that we didn't have fireworks? We didn't go into Mr Giovanni's shop to get those chocolates? None of it was real? We just saw what you were thinking? This "mind-touching" thing?'

I don't wait for the answer. There isn't one. Not one that's going to make sense. 'OK, what about the chocolates? I took the box home. Me and my mum *ate* them. They were delicious.'

'No, you only thought you d-did. That's how real mind-touching is. If you go and take a l-look in Mr Giovanni's shop window, you'll find—'

'I know what I'll find, Reggie, I've already been there.'

'W-well, then?'

'Well then, nothing. What about the fireworks?'

'The same. They never happened, not for real. That's why there were n-no cases left.'

'And you did all these things, right? You made fireworks appear in the sky and a number appear on a lolly stick?'

He suddenly looks at me, surprised, as if I've missed the point. 'No, not m-me, Alice.'

Now I'm getting cross. 'But you said you did it.'

'No, I said I c-*could* do it. But it's not me who's been doing it. Don't you realize?' He stops. Looks hard at me. 'It's not me. It's you.'

That really is it. I've had it now. The anger is boiling. A thermometer in my mouth would read 'danger of explosion; remove from mouth'.

'You're cracked, Reggie. You're cracked! I didn't do anything. Don't you think I'd know if I could go around doing things like that?'

'That's how mind-touching starts. You do it without even knowing it. You just think you're thinking really hard about things. People do that all the time, but with us something else happens and suddenly you're showing people what's in your mind, what you want them to see, and they think it's real. That's what happened to Denis that day by the canal; he saw what you were thinking. That's why he ran away. And then with the chewing gum: it was you doing it. You made the Spicers think they were caught up in gum because that's what you wanted to happen.'

I cut across him. 'All right. What about the tidal wave? D'you really think I was trying to drown myself on that lake?'

His expression changes. He looks worried.

'I've been thinking a lot about that. There must be someone else around, apart from us, who can d-do it too and whoever it is is obviously trying to f-frighten us.'

If my mum were here, she'd say, 'He's taken leave of his senses.' He's certainly taken leave of something.

'I see. 'Course. And who is this mysterious person? Anybody I know? Let me guess . . . it was Norman. No,

Denis Spicer. No, don't tell me, I've got it . . . Mrs Gilbey! On her way to collect her pension, she thought she'd have a bit of fun mind-touching and scaring us to death at the same time. This is mad, and so are you! Things like this only happen in books, and it's called magic, and it's not real.'

'Alice, this has got nothing to do with m-magic.'

'So what *has* it got to do with? That makes any sense, that is.'

'It's to do with being able to do something special and . . . '

'Don't start all that barmy stuff again.'

'It's not b-barmy. I know how you're feeling. I used to think I was the only one who could do it. It scared me so I didn't tell anyone. But when we came here I could feel there was someone close by who could do it too. First time I saw you, I knew it was you. But then I realized it wasn't just you. I was getting these b-bad feelings too. I think it must be someone who's close to you, knows you well. Knows where you go, what you do.'

'Yeah, my bloody shadow. Look, if you're gonna keep this up I'm going home.'

'I know how it s-sounds, but it's all true.'

I start to walk away. 'Yeah, right. Tell it to the fairies. You know, the ones at the bottom of your garden; the garden with the gnome in it who pulls rabbits out of a hat.'

I hear him calling my name. Don't turn round. I keep going. Head down. The way I always walk when I've got something on my mind. Can't stand to be inside. Shut up. I just walk, nowhere, anywhere. The wind blows through my mind, shakes up my thoughts like leaves on trees. Scatters them. I try to pick them up. But I can't. I walk and walk. Can't get anything straight. The wind blows.

## ★★★ 15 Shakespeare, scientists and Geronimo

I come here when I need to talk to someone who's going to listen. If anyone can help, Mrs Gilbey can. She used to look after me when I was a little girl and my mum was working. She lives in one of the posh houses around the corner. They're not joined to lots of other houses in a block like ours. Hers is big, with high ceilings, and lovely windows in the front that let in as much light as you could ever want. Inside there are lots of doors that must lead to lots of rooms. I knock. Hear her in the hallway.

'Hello, Alice. What a nice surprise. Come in. I'm just making some tea.'

She always seems pleased to see me, makes me feel special. She leads me into a room that sparkles like a new pin, pink roses on the wallpaper – beats our green mould.

Nothing ever seems to change here. There's a tall, shiny coal scuttle, full of real coal, not the tarry block wood that we use in our fire. And there's so much furniture: a settee and an armchair with lacy things on the backs, a chest of drawers so shiny you can see your face in it, with patterns carved in the wood. It smells of polish. On top of the chest is a clutter of photographs: men with moustaches, white-shirted, in baggy trousers. And smiling women, sleek as film stars, dressed like princesses, arm in arm with the men – linked for ever.

I turn to look at Mrs Gilbey, carefully, the way Sherlock Holmes would. Only my magnifying glass is imaginary. She's a small, neat bundle of blue and white. The white is her blouse and her hair – except her hair's more silver than white. The blue is her skirt. And she has a blue brooch with a white swan painted on it. Blue is her favourite colour. Even her eyes are blue.

'I'll just put the kettle on.'

She goes out. I hear a tap running. Cupboard doors open and close. She comes back in with a tray, balances a teapot the shape of a thatched cottage, two thin white cups and saucers with pink swirly patterns, and a plate of cakes.

'We'll just let the tea draw for a minute.'

I imagine a teapot drawing a picture.

'So, how are you?'

'All right, Emma . . . ' I call her Emma when we're on our own. If my mum knew she'd tell me off.

'There's a "but" waiting to get out there, if I'm not much mistaken.'

'It's Reggie.'

She pours the tea – a golden stream. Offers me the plate of cakes. My mum has always told me that if I ever eat in anyone else's house I shouldn't take the biggest piece and I should always leave a bit on my plate. Funny, here I am with all this going on and I think of that.

'Go on, then.'

I take a deep breath and tell her the whole story.

She doesn't say a word. Just keeps looking at me. Listens to every word.

When I've finished, she sits back. She thinks for a while, then gets up and goes to the window. I expected her to be really surprised. She's not.

'Oh, dear.'

'It *is* all rubbish, Emma, isn't it?'

She takes a long time to answer. 'Well . . . you've got to remember, dear, that Reggie hasn't had things easy. He doesn't have a mum or dad. He seems to have moved around a lot, and he's often had to change schools. Let's face it, he is bound to have . . . ' She stops. Still looking out of the window as if she'll find the words there, she continues, ' . . . problems.'

She stops again. I don't say anything. Something's telling me I need to listen carefully.

'Reggie is a lonely young man, Alice. He hasn't a friend in the world apart from you – and thank goodness he's got you, that's all I can say – but he's still got the same needs we all have. Reggie wants to be loved, to have people think that he's special. It sounds to me as if what he's been doing is more about trying to get himself noticed than it is about magic or making impossible things happen. I'd say it's about impressing you. Your friendship is the most important thing in the world to him. If he can persuade you that this mind-touching business is real then he'll be special in your eyes and he'll do anything to be that.'

'But he said that I could do it too. That I was doing it without even knowing it.'

'Well, he would say that, love, wouldn't he? If you're doing it too then you're both in it together. Blood brothers. Comrades in arms. You know something the rest of us don't. You can both do something we can't – it ties the two of you together. And the reason you don't know you're doing it is simple: you're not.'

'And what about this other person who can do it, the one who's trying warn us off, to scare us?'

'Same thing. If someone is trying to scare you both it makes the bond between you two even stronger. You're the goodies, they're the baddies. As we used to say in my young day, it's you two against the world.'

She comes back to the chair. Picks up her tea. Stays standing.

My brain is telling me she's right. But my words sound as if I want Reggie to be telling the truth. I don't know why that is.

'But all those things I told you about. I was there. I saw them happen.'

She looks at me almost sharply.

'Did you, Alice?'

It's more of a challenge than a question. Then her voice softens. 'Did you really?'

She looks at me.

'You're an imaginative girl. You write stories, create other worlds. You put people in them and make them do and say whatever it is you want them to do and say. I bet you even believe your characters are real sometimes, don't you? People with minds like yours can sometimes see things that aren't there. There's nothing wrong in that, dear. You just have a very active imagination. It's a gift, but like all gifts you've got to learn how to use it properly. You've got to learn to tell fact from fiction, reality from fantasy. It's about growing up, my love. Sooner or later we all have to do that.'

'But what about the fireworks? You saw 'em yourself.'

'Of course I did.'

'But we didn't have any! The Spicers nicked 'em.'

'Stole, Alice.'

'Sorry. The Spicers stole 'em.'

'So you want to know where Reggie got them from? Well, he could have found them. A lot of people have fireworks. Maybe someone just dropped them. Maybe not. He could have been saving secretly. Maybe he even took them from the shop.'

'You mean he ni— stole them?'

'It's possible.'

'All right. So why weren't there any used cases? I looked everywhere. There wasn't a single one.'

'Perhaps one of your friends collects dead firework cases – people do the strangest things – and if I remember rightly, didn't it snow the day after bonfire night? It was beautiful. I love snow, it puts the world to sleep under a blanket. But blankets also cover things up, don't they? I should think that most of the firework cases were covered by the snow.'

I think back. She's right. It did snow that morning. And the snow got heavier as I was going back to our bomb site to look for the cases.

'But what about the tidal wave? And the boat? It just started to row itself. Honest, Emma.'

'A summer storm would be my guess. They often come from nowhere and go the same way. When there's thunder and lightning it can be terrifying. Perhaps there was a strong wind and it just blew the boat along.'

'But the boat was rocking. We nearly sank!'

'Now, this is only an idea – I could be wrong – but is it possible that Reggie was deliberately rocking the boat?' She pauses, giving me time to think. 'Maybe he just saw the storm coming behind you in the sky – sometimes they do bring very high winds – and he started rocking the boat. It got dark. The water got choppy. You got scared. Then the storm blew over and he stopped rocking. There one minute, gone the next. He just made it seem more frightening than it was. He knows full well what you're like. How you can get a bit carried away at times.'

'You mean he deliberately scared the life out of me just so that I'd think someone was trying to get us?'

'You mustn't think badly of him. Not you of all people.

You must remember he's doing these things for you: to impress you. So you'll be his friend.'

'But I don't want to be impressed. All right, what about that day by the canal? Reggie said that Denis ran away because he could see what I was thinking, see something horrible about to happen to him.'

'Maybe . . . or maybe Denis just saw someone he knew up on the bridge: his dad probably. I do know those boys live in fear of their dad. Denis knew he shouldn't have been out of school, and got scared in case he was in trouble.'

'And the bubble gum machine?'

'It could be that the pavement under the machine was just uneven. There's a lot of traffic using that road these days; lorries on their way to the docks. Maybe a lorry went by and the vibrations tipped the gum machine over. Then that good old imagination of yours took over. There are so many ifs, perhapses and maybes, my love, and they're all more likely explanations than the mind-touching one Reggie's trying to get you to believe.'

She sips her tea. I do the same. Mine has gone cold.

'Friends should stand by each other, but they should also know about each other, otherwise you don't know what it is that you're standing by.' She smiles. 'Oh dear, does that sound confusing?'

'I know what you mean.'

She pauses.

'Reggie's not a bad boy; in many ways he's a good person. But even good people can use other people for their own ends. Even good people have problems.'

I feel as if I've been run over by a trolleybus. My brain is flattened. But something inside me carries on. Like I have to defend Reggie. Like I want him to be telling the truth.

'And the lolly stick? The lucky number? You think that's just a trick?'

My eyes dare her to answer. It takes her a long time.

'I don't know, love. Maybe he somehow found out what the number was and he already had a stick hidden somewhere with the number written on it. Perhaps he knows how to make invisible ink?'

I interrupt. 'But why?'

'It's like I said, Alice. He knows how imaginative you are – he's playing on it.

'But the chocolates! We went back and got them. It was just like I told you.'

'Except in the morning there was nothing to show that it had ever happened. You don't even have the box. It's still in the window. The same box: the one with the mark on the ribbon. You said so yourself.'

'Yes, but . . . '

'There's no such thing as magic, Alice. Except in your imagination. I suppose the better your imagination, the more magic you can see.'

'D'you think I'm lying? About what I saw, I mean?'

'Alice, I've known you since you were three. I know

you don't lie. You've told me exactly what you think you saw. What you wanted to see.' She pauses. 'With Reggie's help.'

She puts down her cup and saucer, looks straight at me. 'Reggie has just played a few tricks. Maybe when he's good and ready he'll tell you that it was just a bit of fun. Although I think by now he's probably even managed to convince himself it's all real. My mother used to say that if you tell a lie often enough you believe it yourself. Whatever, all he really did was to buy some fireworks you didn't know about, put invisible ink on a lolly stick, and make a summer storm into a hurricane. Your imagination did the rest. I bet you even dreamed about it.'

She was right, I did. Tidal waves chasing chocolates; Mr Giovanni in a rowing boat; the number twenty-seven written in the sky.

I nod.

'Well then, when you woke up, the dream became reality. You convinced yourself you had got the chocolates and eaten them. You even thought you'd still have the box. But you didn't.' She takes hold of my hand. 'It's all part of the same thing. It's a great story, though. Mind-touching – good name. I don't know about you, but I'm certainly impressed. Unfortunately, not in the way Reggie probably wants.'

I take a deep breath. It all begins to make sense. The more I listen, the more I know she's right. I don't know whether to laugh or cry, to be happy or disappointed.

'Don't forget your friendship means an awful lot to Reggie.'

'But he's tricked me! Lied to me!'

'No, my love. That's the whole point.' She's still holding my hand. She looks straight into my eyes as if this is really important. 'In his head it may well be that it's all happening, just as he says it is. It's a bit like an echo. He shouted and it bounced back off you. You both heard it and shared in it. In that way you're encouraging each other. There's nothing wrong in that, Alice. It's like I said before. As long as you understand how echoes work.'

She stops and thinks for a while. 'Some American Indian tribes thought echoes were the voices of their ancestors calling them. Scientists just talk about sound vibrations. The Indians believe they are right and so do the scientists. Can anyone really say who *is* right?' She picks up the teapot. It steams from the spout. Hot. Comforting. There's a look in her eyes. 'Reggie is on the side of the Indians. Now give me your cup and I'll pour you another.'

Then, as she's pouring the tea, she shivers.

'You all right, Emma?'

'I think so, dear. Someone walking over my grave. I suddenly thought of something I read as a young girl – I must have been about your age – Shakespeare, I think. Now what on earth could have put that into my head? I haven't thought about that in ages. How did it go? Something like: "*There are more things in heaven and earth, Horatio, than are dreamed of in your philosophy.*"'

She looks up, and there's a puzzled expression on her face. It makes my stomach wobble.

'What does that mean?'

'It means that in spite of everything I've just said there is always the chance that I could be wrong; that what Reggie is telling you is true. Wouldn't that be a turn-up for the books?' Her expression doesn't change. 'In which case, you have to decide which side you're on, Alice. Which is it to be? The scientists or the Indians?'

Suddenly I feel scared.

# ★★★ 16 Nursery rhymes and breaking ice

The weeks are passing. The nights are lighter now. The days are warmer. I haven't seen Reggie for a while. I still like him, I always will, but I need to be away from him. When I'm with him it's like being in a mad dream. And who wants to live in a mad dream?

It feels more normal with my old friends. The way things should be. No one pretending they can do impossible stuff. The only magic we can do is disappearing when the teachers want us.

Things are even a bit better at home. Bert knows I'm not seeing Reggie so he's leaving me alone most of the time, and he and Mum are really happy what with the new baby coming.

The play is coming along really well too. When I'm writing I can forget everything that's going on, lose myself. Sister Bernadette said we should try to get some scenery because that will make it more believable. She wants us to organize the whole thing. Scary! So we have to write the programmes, sort out the costumes, design the tickets, everything.

In the play I'm still turning things upside down. Watson's the clever one, although Holmes still acts as if *he* is. Veronica is really great as Watson, she's so funny. George is finding Holmes a bit difficult. He's learned most of the words, but he's just not natural at it like Veronica. Still, we're all different. We're going to get him a real violin to play. That should be interesting.

Most dinner times we bolt our food down, then head for the hall to rehearse. The word seems to have got around. We were only going to have a few characters, but now there are more kids than parts. I don't mind – I'll just write in a few more characters. You have to watch out that it doesn't mess up the storyline when you do that, though.

We've just arrived in the hall again, waiting to start, George pretending to play the piano. I look up to see Reggie standingat the door, looking in. He just stands there, chewing one ofhis nails. I know I shouldn't, but I still feel angry with him.Then I remind myself what Mrs Gilbey said – that it's not his fault – and smile.

Josephine Murphy is saying her words now, she's little Miss Muffet. In the play, instead of being terrified of spiders she acts out of character by really loving them and letting them crawl all over her. I'm trying to get her to say her words a bit louder.

Reggie's moved from outside the hall. Now he's standing just inside the door. I concentrate on Miss Muffet for a while, but when I look around again he's gone.

After break we go back to class. Much as I try to think

about other things, I can't get Reggie out of my mind. It's like he's got himself a little corner there, and every now and then comes out and just won't go away. Maybe he should take the part of Little Jack Horner in the play. The thought makes me smile.

When the bell goes for the end of the day and I walk outside, he's waiting for me, sitting on the gate across the road. He's got a piece of string dangling from his hand. Flash is jumping up trying to catch it. I can see he's not sure what to say. He fiddles with the string – nervous. I feel sorry for him. Must be terrible to feel you have to make up a load of lies to look big.

'What you doing?'

'W-waiting for you.'

'What for?'

'Thought we c-could walk home together.'

There's this long silence like neither of us know what to say. After what seems a long time he says,'I thought the p-play was good. Veronica's excellent as Doctor Watson.'

'Thanks.'

'What's the m-mystery Holmes has to solve?'

'He has to work out why the all the characters have stopped behaving like they should. Prince Charming can't wake Sleeping Beauty with a kiss. Popeye is frightened of his own shadow. Humpty Dumpty refuses to fall off the wall. Jack and Jill won't go up the hill and get water, and little Miss Muffet likes spiders.'

Reggie laughs. 'That's g-great.'

'So Sherlock Holmes gets called in to sort things out.'

'Good old Sherlock Holmes. We could d-do with him ourselves.'

I nod. Don't say anything. We start to walk home together.

'What you going to d-do now?'

'Get some bread and jam, then I've got to go to the gasworks to get some tarry blocks for the fire.'

That's a job I hate doing. I'm sure that's why Bert makes me do it. I have to take this battered old pram and get it filled with these wooden blocks we burn on the fire. I hate it, mainly because I always bump into loads of kids I know from school. It's like they've been waiting around, just so they can bump into me. They always look in the pram, take the mickey and make these really unfunny comments about what a weird-looking baby or some such stuff. Bert came by once when a load of boys I didn't know were all standing around making fun. For a minute I thought he was going to sort them out. He just walked past though, didn't say anything.

'I'll c-come with you. I like the gasworks.'

'Reggie, you're such a dimwit. *Nobody* likes the gasworks. All right, tell you what. I'll let you come if you push the pram.'

'Great.'

Great? Pushing a pram? You're such a case!

We go home most of the way together. Reggie stays out on the street while I go inside to get some bread and jam and the old pram. We've got to be careful. If Bert thought I was seeing him again there'd be hell to pay.

I push open the door. He's sitting there. A cigarette burns on the edge of the table. I didn't expect him to be home. My heart jumps. I step back for an instant. He grins.

'What's the matter with you?' He picks up the cigarette. Taps ash on to the floor. 'Jumpy as a cat on a roof.'

I look away quick. Feel my cheeks flame. Keep my head down. Pray that Reggie stays outside.

He laughs but it's not a real laugh. It's hollow. Something black inside.

'Don't forget those blocks for the fire or I'll give you something to be nervous about.'

He puts the cigarette to his lips, smoke breathes out through his nose.

I get the bread and jam as fast as I can. I can feel him watching me all the time. Not saying anything. Just watching. I get as much jam on my sleeve as I do on the bread.

I stuff the sandwiches into my pocket and hurry out, back to Reggie. I look back, can't help myself, but there's no one there. We're safe.

The sky is flat and grey, like it's forgotten it's the sky and thinks it's the sea. We cross Commercial Road and go down Watney Street towards the gasworks and under the railway arch. I've never been on a train – I'd love to go on a train, to the countryside on a bright summer's day. We pass the pie and mash shop. The smell of the pies cooking drifts out.

'I saw your m-mum the other day.'

I wonder if he's trying to get back to all the normal stuff. Maybe he's realized that I'm not going to believe what he says just because he says it.

'Did you?'

'By the sweet factory down by the canal.'

'She works there now, part time. Think she's saving up money for the new baby. She fetches some of the sweets home sometimes. They're sort of like toffee with Brazil nuts in it.'

'I like Brazil n-nuts.'

'I'll save you some next time she gets any.'

'Thanks.'

'Only problem is she has to sneak them out in her apron pocket, so they have bits of fluff stuck to them.'

'Is she s-stealing them?'

'Perk of the job, she says. They ain't gonna miss a few sweets, are they?'

'No, I s'pose not, they've got m-millions of them.'

'D'you think if you owned the factory you'd be eating your own sweets all day?'

'No.'

'Why?'

'Because all my t-teeth would fall out.' He covers his teeth with his lips. 'Like thish.'

'You're barmy.'

We pass the high wall that surrounds the gasworks.

Afternoon shadows drift out. I don't see it at first. A shadow turns into a figure. The figure leaps out from behind the wall, a black balaclava hiding his face. He's got a wooden gun in his hand. Makes me jump.

'Gotcha. Surrender or die.'

At the moment I need Norman like I need a kiss from Gary Spicer.

'You gotta stop doin' that, Norman. You're gonna give someone a heart attack.'

'Put your hands up.'

'Not now, Norman. I'm not in the mood.'

'Who are you, friend or foe?'

'The Queen.'

'Let's see your identity papers then, Your Majesty.'

I search in my pocket. Give him an old bus ticket.

'You're not the Queen. You're the number 48 to Aldgate.'

'My mistake.'

'Wh-where you off to, Norm?'

'See my uncle.'

I notice he has a black armband on.

'What's that for?'

'My uncle. He got knocked down by a lorry. My mum says I've got to go and play my last respects.'

'What does that mean, Norm?'

'Dunno. Think he must have been in a band. Where you two goin' anyway?'

Reggie grins. 'Some German spies are hiding in the old

gasworks. We're going to flush them out.'

I say, 'Get some tarry blocks for the fire.'

Norm winks at Reggie, 'Watch out for snipers.'

Across the road the pub doors open. A group of old ladies come out laughing. He tosses a grenade at them. They explode into fragments of bloomers and fox stoles. One of them puts up her umbrella and Tommy-guns Norman to death. He dies groaning. A hero. She laughs so hard her teeth fall out.

Norman looks up, 'Here, Alice – just remembered; my cousin Frankie wants to be in the play.'

'We still need a Prince Charming.'

I don't tell Norman that none of the boys want to be Prince Charming.

'Who's Prince Charming when he's at home?'

'He's a really important character. He starts it all off really, because he kisses Sleeping Beauty but she doesn't wake up like she's does in the real story.'

Norman looks interested, 'Kisses?'

'That's right. He has to kiss Sleeping Beauty.'

'Isn't Kathy O'Brien Sleeping Beauty?'

'Yeah.'

'So this Prince Charming bloke gets to kiss Kathy O'Brien?'

'Sleeping Beauty, Norman. She's Kathy O'Brien in the playground.'

'I know that, Alice, but she won't let anyone kiss her there.'

'She does in the play.'

He gets up. Brushes himself down.

'I'd be a really good prince bloke. Don't you think?'

'You are good-looking, in your balaclava.'

'Thanks, Alice. And I reckon Frankie would be a good Humpty Dumpty.'

'W-why's that, Norm?'

'He likes scrambled eggs.'

'R-right.'

'So, I'll be the prince then.'

'If you're sure.'

'Yeah, sure. See you.'

We watch him march off.

'I'd like to be with him when he p-plays his last respects.'

We both laugh, and suddenly I'm putting on my ice skates and hoping the ice isn't going to break. I suppose it was bound to happen. You can't keep walking around the edges of a friendship, afraid to test it. True friends have to bear each other's weight, if you see what I mean.

'I saw Mrs Gilbey the other day. I was telling her about all this mind-touching stuff you've been going on about.'

'I thought you m-might.'

'She thinks that you're making it all up, to impress me. To make sure we stay friends.'

Part of me is hoping he's just going to say yes, she's right, I'm sorry, it was just a bit of fun, I was just teasing you a bit. Another part knows he isn't. He doesn't say anything. I try again.

'You don't have to do anything to impress me, you know. No magic tricks. No fantastic stories.'

He doesn't stop, but slows down. His voice changes a bit.

'It's not a story. I'm not doing any t-tricks. Something's happening and we're caught in the middle of it.'

I feel sorry for him. I'm beginning to think that he really does believe all this rubbish.

We reach the tarry block factory. There's a bit of a queue in front of us. An old lady starts shouting – something about the last lot of tarry blocks being rubbish – tells the man she's going to see the boss or something. Then she turns, nearly knocks me over, and slams out. The man mutters something after her. Looks up, scowls at us. He's only got two teeth.

'What d'you kids want?'

Funny how adults do that. Here we are, standing in the tarry block queue, and he asks us that.

'Two portions of jellied eels, please.'

'Don't be so cheeky, you.'

I give him my money. He pushes the ticket at me.

We go back outside and give our ticket to another man – he's the one who gives you the blocks. He takes it. Doesn't say anything. Starts to shovel the blocks into sacks. Every now and again he straightens up, rubs his back, moans and looks at us as if it's our fault he's got a backache. He looks at the pram, looks at me, sneers. I stare back at him, tempted to poke my tongue out. But I remind myself I'm not a baby, and do a rude sign behind my back instead. That'll teach him!

Reggie takes the pram. We walk back. He seems to want to talk.

'I know it doesn't m-make sense to you yet. I f-felt like that at first. When I was growing up in that children's home I was always scared, frightened of my own sh-shadow. My stutter was really bad then. No one knew what I was talking about half the time. When I started mind-touching I got more confident. It was scary, but at the same time it made me feel I could do things the other kids couldn't. It might help you too, with things.'

'What things?'

He looks straight back at me. 'Your stepd-dad.'

'What you talking about now?'

'It might help you sort things out. F-face up to him.'

I turn away but he's still looking at me. I feel tears prick my eyes, but I'm not going to cry. I'm not going to let anyone see. Not even Reggie. Inside, though, I get angry. Maybe it's because he said what he did. Maybe I'm ashamed that he knows. Maybe I'm just confused. He's telling me one thing, Mrs Gilbey's telling me another. The only thing I know for sure is that I feel mixed up.

Then that horrible little voice that lives in my head wakes up again.

'I can sort out whatever I want to and I don't need any help from anyone to do it. If you want to do something useful you could start by stopping all this. I've had enough of all your stories. You're a liar, Reggie. A bloody liar.'

It's out before I can stop it. He looks at me. Really sad, like.

Here we go again. Why did I have to say that? Somewhere I hear the loud crack of breaking ice.

# ⋆⋆⋆ 17 Nan

I swing my legs out of bed, and it's there straight away in my head – I feel terrible about Reggie. Maybe he does think he's telling me the truth about what's happening. Maybe that's what's so scary. It's the truth as he sees it. But does that make it *really* true? I don't know. I just don't know. I'm sorry for calling him a liar, though. Sorry for losing my temper.

The floor is cold. Numbs my feet. Things are going from bad to worse.

I pull on my clothes untidily, knowing Mum is not in the kitchen burning porridge on to the bottom of the saucepan. She had to go into hospital last week. The doctor said she needed to rest, otherwise there might be a problem with the baby. I don't like it when Mum's away. If only she were here I'd eat the porridge, burned bits and all, and open the window so I could hear her singing.

What's even worse, my nan is here. Bert told me I have to call her Nan. I said I would, but most of the time I don't. She came as soon as Mum went into hospital. She's not like the sweet old nans you read about in books. She's old but she's got jet-black hair, pulled back, an inky outline around her head. Sharp eyes. Long, thin nose. Cardigan sleeves rolled up. Small and skinny with a blurred tattoo on her arm. Skin so thin if you held her up to the light you'd see right through her. Grey eyes just like Bert.

She keeps brown powder in a little silver tin. Pinches it out. Puts a bit on to the back of her hand and sniffs it up loudly. Her nose is powdered brown from one pinch too many. Mum told me it's snuff – ground-up tobacco. Fancy putting ground-up tobacco up your nose! Mind you, fancy putting it in paper and smoking it.

Sometimes, when she sees me looking at her, she says, 'D'you wanna pinch?' Then she grins wickedly and offers the box as a challenge.

She's sleeping on a camp-bed in the other half of the bedroom, and she keeps a candle burning all night. It throws up giant shadows as she moves. When she gets up in the night to go to the lavatory I watch her witch's shadow on the curtain. Sometimes I wake up and I'm sure she's watching me. Just like Bert does. I wish she'd go back home.

I'm gonna be late for school. I try to clear up as best I can. Wish I'd done it last night. I make it to school. Wish I hadn't. Get most of my maths wrong and get into trouble for talking during a test. Miss Lacey seems really cross. I don't want to be there. Trouble is, I'm not sure *where* I want to be, so I wander around on my own in the playground.

The day's a blur. Glad when it's over. Only thing is, I don't want to go home. It feels strange there without Mum. So I wander around until I'm so hungry and tired it's the only thing I can do.

I walk home slowly, turn into the passage and decide to go straight to my room. A noise stops me. Loud banging and muffled shouts are coming from the end of the passage near our room. I move closer. It's coming from the lavatory. For a second I wonder what's going on. Then I realize. Someone is stuck in there. I listen; it's Nan's voice.

There's a piece of wood wedged under the door. It could have been kicked under there accidentally by someone taking a short cut through the flats then out the back yard door to the bomb site. It could even have been shoved under by some kids, out to play a trick on someone.

I bend down to pick it up, and I can't help myself, I just have to laugh. Then I hear footsteps behind me.

'What's going on?'

I turn around. It's him. I pull out the wood. The door bursts open and Nan stumbles out. Her hair is all over the place. Her face red. She looks at me. We both look at the piece of wood in my hand. She puts two and two together and gets the sum wrong.

'You wicked girl!'

'But . . . '

He has his coat over his shoulder. 'What's she done now?' His voice sounds cold and hard.

She repeats the question. 'What's she done?' She sounds

like a parrot. 'I'll tell you what she's done. I've been in there for hours. Locked in! You know I can't stand to be locked in anywhere. Laughing, she was. I heard her!' Says it as if it's a crime. Guilty of laughing. She looks at me again, her eyes narrowed. 'She needs sorting out, that one.'

I can't believe what's happening.

'It wasn't me! I heard you callin' out. There was a piece of wood stuck under the door. I just took it away.'

She sniffs disbelievingly, her pointed nose seems even sharper.

'She was laughing. I could hear her.'

'Sorry. It just seemed funny. Nan stuck in the lav.'

But I'm appealing to something that isn't there. Neither of them could see a joke if it came up, said, 'Hello, I'm a joke', and bit them on the bum. I wonder why she's making so much fuss. She spends hours in there anyway. Takes her newspaper and a tin of snuff in every morning. I can hear her turning the pages while I pace up and down outside with my legs crossed like a bow-legged chicken, dying for a wee.

I should have saved my breath. She doesn't believe me.

The trouble is I want to laugh again. I have this picture of whoever did it creeping down the corridor. A secret agent, spying out the land. Then, when the coast is clear, while she's getting comfortable with her paper, quietly wedging the wood under the door. Mission accomplished. Enemy captured.

Perhaps it was Norman, on a military exercise into

no-man's land. Orders to capture little old ladies in lavatories. No, it couldn't have been Norman. He wouldn't have used a bit of old wood. He'd have used barbed wire and land mines.

I know I shouldn't find it funny. For one thing it's really cold in there: an icebox. But even that thought paints another picture in my head – Nan's bottom in a block of ice. The more pictures I see, the more difficult it is not to laugh. The harder I try not to, the more I want to. I hold my breath. My stomach hurts.

She gives him a look. 'You need to sort her out. Now.'

'But I didn't do anything!'

'You calling me a liar too, are you?'

'No.' I appeal to her. 'Did you see who did it?'

'How could I? I was inside.'

'Then how d'you know it was me?' She scowls at me. Mutters to herself, 'In that lav for hours, I was.'

The words slink into my head. Slide in. Grinning Cheshire cats of words. Lining up to make me laugh. Digging each other in the ribs. They sing to me:

*Oh dear, what can the matter be?*

*Bert's old mum got stuck in the lavatory,*

*She's been there from Monday to Saturday—*

The dam bursts. I give a little, nervous strangled laugh.

She glares. 'There, see what I mean. She needs someone to teach her a lesson, that young missie. Too much old cheek if you ask me.' She looks hard at him, then sort of smiles at me. It's not a nice smile. 'A proper lesson, I mean.'

He looks at me. His eyes bore into me.

'You're never going to learn, are you? No respect. Always looking down your nose, thinking you're better than the rest of us. Always trying to be something you ain't.'

It's so unfair that I can't help it; I answer back. 'I don't think I'm better than anybody. And I'm not trying to be anything, except me.'

I mean my voice to sound brave and strong. It doesn't. He moves towards me. I move back. Trouble is the wall's behind me. He pushes his face up close, his eyes strike like lances into mine.

'Get to your room. I'll deal with you later, once I've had a chance to calm the old lady down. Now get.'

There's something in his voice. I don't argue. I'm glad to get away.

I lie on my bed. Somehow, suddenly, it doesn't seem so funny any more. I suppose I'll have to stay here all night.

Outside I can hear them talking, but I don't want to hear what they're saying. I pull the blanket over my head. My bed's a galleon with sails billowing in the bright, strong wind and I'm sailing away, far out to sea on foam-flecked, white-capped waves. And on the distant horizon sea birds wheel, and I can see the sandy white shoreline of some island and I know there'll be no one there except . . . ?

The door slams. I start. Must have dozed off. Through the window I can see it's dark. I try to screw up my eyes tighter and look out through them at the same time. I sense someone standing there. The curtain moves, letting in a fuzz of yellow light from the lamp outside, taking the edge off the darkness. He stands silhouetted against the light, a large, flat black shape.

I try not to move. I screw up my eyes. Pretend to be asleep. I get that feeling, sick in my stomach. I can smell that smell. Stale. Beery. Heavy. He's unsteady. Stumbles against the bed.

He moves towards me, and I know what's coming. It's been a while, but I feel my muscles tighten. My fingers bunch. My mouth becomes dry.

I open one eye. He's standing there, tapping something against the palm of his hand. As I watch, his arm goes up. Something snakes high into the air. I watch it against the light from the window. It coils back behind him, uncoils, freezes for an instant. Then it lashes down. His hard leather belt bites into my back like an animal attacking me.

'I've had just about enough of you . . . ' His voice rasps. 'Maybe this'll learn you . . . ' Again the belt goes up. 'Give you something . . . ' Comes stinging down. ' . . . to think about . . . '

I try to get away. Hear myself cry out as it catches me across the shoulders.

Again the belt goes up and comes down in time with what he's saying. As if there's a link between the belt and the words. As if the words are the belt.

I roll over to protect myself. Fall off the bed. I call out. Ask him to stop. Hear the panic in my voice. Still it goes on. It seems like now there's no belt any more, and it's the words that are eating into me. Words and pain mingle together. Harder and faster. Harder and faster. Like the world is fixed in a mad rhythm, keeping time to the pain on my back. I'm aware of myself huddled into a ball on the floor. Against the clear, night sky through the window the belt goes up again. Black against the silver full moon. I wait for it to come down.

Then all of a sudden anger floods through me, like a pulse in the darkness of my head. And from the anger, I get that feeling, something soft as down brushing against my cheek. It only lasts an instant then goes. I see him moving to hit me again. I see the belt change. It's not a belt any more. His arm rises again. It sweeps up. I wait for it to come down. But this time the belt doesn't snap down on me. It twists back. Coils. A black tongue forks the air. Hisses a warning. It has a life of its own now. It twists around his arm, flicks up to his face, knots its long body around his neck. I hear him shout. He's frightened. He grabs at it, tries to throw it away. And now I can see the snake's body tightening its grip around his neck. He's fighting for breath. I can hear him panting; know he can't breathe. His scream pierces me.

The images in my head shatter. Suddenly, the belt drops from his hand and falls to the floor.

There's a terrible silence. He looks from me to the belt and back again. His eyes are blank. Shaking, he turns and stumbles from the room.

I slowly pull myself back on to my bed. Stay curled in a ball. Try to find a place to lie on that isn't sore. I lie motionless, feeling the stinging pain in my back.

I sleep, badly.

In the morning the belt's still there. Flat, lifeless on the floor. Just a belt. It all seems like a bad dream, except the marks on my back are real enough. I look at them in the mirror. Angry red weals. Criss-cross pain.

I get out of bed slowly, trying to make sense of what's going on. I'm ordinary. Never been anything else. I'm used to things making sense. Did I really make him see what I wanted him to see? Or was that just some mad dream. My good old overactive imagination. I don't know. I just want to get up. Get out. Away.

## ★★★ 18 Finding out

The bus stop is already heavy with people. I feel terrible, like I haven't slept for a week. The sun is bright. High in a blue sky. Ragged clouds become angels. Chase each other. Play catch on the way to heaven.

I've got a lot of thinking to do. It's been a week now since the belt thing happened and I still feel scared. I seem to be like this all the time now. It's like I'm not me any more. Don't know what to think. What to believe. What's going to happen next. It's like things have got out of control. I'm just watching my life, not really in it.

Nan wasn't there when I woke up. All her stuff was gone. I'm glad. Bert's never at home now either. I wonder if it's anything to do with the other night. Suits me. I couldn't stand the way he keeps looking at me, like he's trying to look inside me, always staring. Weighing me up. Working me out. It scares me. What does he want? Trouble is he's got this habit of turning up when you least expect him.

I'm not going to tell anyone about the belt yet. Not even Reggie. I need time to think about all this. Sort it out. I'll be all right on my own until Mum gets back. I really miss her, and I can't help feeling there's something they're not telling me.

'You all right, dear?'

Mrs Gilbey looks uncomfortable. Pink-faced. Dewy-lipped. Dabs a handkerchief. Doesn't seem to be herself. I nod and smile, but inside I'm nervous. I shouldn't be. After all, it's only my mum we're visiting in hospital and she's not really even ill or anything.

'I bet you'll be glad to see her?'

I nod again.

She fiddles with the rings on her fingers. Twists and turns them. Normally she gives off calm like a slow, shy sea sucking on a sandy beach. Today she seems fidgety.

'Mum is all right, isn't she, Emma?'

She smiles. 'Right as rain.'

She looks at her watch as the number 78 crawls into view. There's a small cheer – then, as we see it's already nearly full, a not-so-small moan. The queue shuffles forward.

'A few little complications, that's all. That's why they've got her in early. Get her resting. Your mum does too much.'

We get to the platform of the bus. I grab the rail and swing on. Hold out my hand to Mrs Gilbey. She takes it and we're on. Downstairs is full. We corkscrew up the sharply winding stairs. Before we can sit down the conductor rings the bell and the bus lurches off. We both half fall into the last two empty seats.

'She needs to get off her feet a bit.'

I nod. Feel guilty, as if it's my fault she doesn't get off her feet a bit. I've got the window seat. Look out and down on the people below.

'It will be different for you when she has the baby and comes home, you know. Babies have a habit of taking over, becoming the centre of attention.'

She says it like it will be a problem, but it won't be. I'm hardly the centre of attention now, so the baby isn't going to make any difference. All the same, the tone of her voice makes me feel uneasy, like she's trying to warn me about something.

The number 78 from Aldgate to Cambridge Heath stops and starts as it hiccups its way to the hospital. Mrs Gilbey looks at her watch too much. The way people do when they're not really looking at the time at all. The conductor whistles up the stairs. Sways expertly to the rhythm of the bus. Dances in perfect time to its movement. Swings down the aisle punching out tickets, calling everybody 'love' or 'mate'.

When Mum told me about the baby it felt odd. As if it was nothing to do with me and she was telling me just to be polite. She didn't seem to be able to find the right words, acted as if it was something complicated. It wasn't. It was simple. She was going to have a baby. I was going to have a brother or sister.

We both sit in silence on the rocking, jerking bus that is tired of being a bus and wants to be a horse in a Wild West rodeo. I expect her to ask me about Reggie. She doesn't. I'm glad, I've gone over every detail I can remember of what has happened since he moved in and came to our school. Turned my mind into a laboratory. Dissected each incident. Put it under the microscope of my memory to see if there are any clues. Any vital piece of information I might have missed. Anything he has said or done that'll help me get to the truth.

I wonder what Sherlock Homes would do in my position. Not much, probably. He was lucky. He only ever had to solve real problems. Track down flesh-and-blood people. I bet no one ever talked to him about mind-touching. All he had to worry about was good old Moriarty, or perhaps that should be bad old Moriarty.

After a few weeks I shut up the laboratory. Give my mind and my memory a rest. Trouble is, you start to remember things that never actually happened. You begin to fit things together that don't fit.

The hospital is a big old Victorian building – a red brickwork cake in a marzipan of grime. I look up. A hundred windows look back down. I wonder which one of those rooms Mum is in.

Mrs Gilbey buys some flowers from a stall. Then we go in and face a warren of angled corridors; a maze of doors and turnings, more doors and more turnings. I know now how a rabbit feels. The smell of cooking hangs like an invisible fog. We wade through yesterday's menus: stale liver and bacon, rice and custard.

Mrs Gilbey knows the way. Clutching the flowers, she walks purposefully until we reach Saint Katherine Ward. She nods at the nurse sitting by the door as we go in, who stops writing and smiles at us.

Mum is lying in a bed at the far end of the ward. Her hair is down, and twists in long curls over the pillow. I feel my step quicken. I want to run. To throw myself at her. I make myself walk. Try not to look at the other patients. Just focus on her.

As I get closer I can see that her eyes are shut. I stop. She looks thinner. Her face is white. Dark shadows underline her eyes, half-moons of tiredness.

The window by her bed is open. A breeze breathes gently in, rearranging the curtains. Mrs Gilbey hushes me with a finger on her lips. On cue, Mum's eyes flicker open. She smiles.

'Hello, love. How are you?' She reaches forward to kiss me. 'Let's have a look at you. My, you've grown.'

I get embarrassed. 'Come off it, Mum. You only saw me three weeks ago.'

'Proper little beauty, isn't she, Emma?'

Mrs Gilbey smiles. Nods. I go red.

'Thanks for bringin' her.' She holds out her hand to me. I take it. Sit by the bed.

Mrs Gilbey says, 'I'll put these in water, Mary.'

Mum sees the flowers. Yellow and white. An armful of sun. 'Oh, you shouldn't have. They're lovely. Cheer the place up.'

Mrs Gilbey goes off in search of a vase and water.

Mum asks the usual questions about school, about me. I feel nervous. Talk too much. I always do when I'm nervous. One of the nurses gives me a look on the way to another patient. Then another on the way back. I stop talking. It suddenly occurs to me that Mrs Gilbey has been gone a long time. Mum moves to sit up. I help her plump up her pillows.

'Thanks, love.' She looks at me. 'Alice . . . ' Stops. Can't make up her mind about something. 'I asked Mrs Gilbey to fetch you in for a reason.' Then, as if she didn't mean it to come out like that, 'I wanted to see you, of course, but there is something else. Something important I need to tell you.' She pats the bed. 'Come and sit closer.'

I do. She strokes my hand.

'Dad wanted me to tell you as soon as I found out I was expecting, but you know how things are. So much to do. Time just runs away with you.' She grins ruefully. 'Thing is, I thought I'd have time. Didn't expect to end up in here. Still, a bit of high blood pressure isn't the end of the world, is it?'

I feel like I'm waiting for something to happen. It's a feeling I don't like. She goes on stroking my hand.

'Then I was going to tell you just before I came in, but that was all a bit of a panic, wasn't it? Still, no excuses. I should have done it before now.'

She's making me feel worried.

'What is it, Mum? Is something wrong?'

'No, nothing's wrong. I'm a bit tired, but that's to be expected.'

Her fingers pick at the edges of the sheet. She fidgets. Doesn't seem to be comfortable. I wonder if my weight on the bed is getting too heavy for her.

'D'you want me to move?'

'No, you're all right. This all took us a bit by surprise, you know. Expect you noticed that.'

She goes quiet. 'The thing is, I was told a long time ago . . .'

She says the words slowly as if I'm doing some exam and she's giving me clues to the answers. 'A long time ago, I had to have an op . . . I was nineteen. Always wanted a big family.' She looks away. 'I got ill, went to see a doctor. I had to go into hospital. They fixed me up all right, but told me that I couldn't have children; that I'd never be able to have a child.'

She stops, as if I should have understood the clues. Passed the exam.

'I was devastated, love. Good word that, devastated, like an end of the world word, ain't it.'

She smiles but it's not a real smile, it's a tired, sad smile.

'When I came out of hospital an old aunt who lived in the country said I could go and stay with her until I got a bit stronger. Kent it was, by the hop fields. Beautiful after all the bombing in London. So quiet and peaceful. And in the next village was an orphanage. Couldn't believe it. There I was next door to all those poor mites. It was then that I had the idea. If I couldn't have kids of my own then I'd work with them, help look after them.'

I feel her hand squeeze mine tightly. Mrs Gilbey has been gone too long.

'I did really well. I was a natural, the matron said, all the kids loved me. So I decided to stay and make a life for myself there. That was me all done and dusted, life planned out, or so I thought.' She stops. Starts talking quickly like she's nervous.

'Then one day they brought you in. You were such a lovely little thing. Red hair, big blue eyes and so cheeky. You'd been caught up in a bombing raid in London. The house was smashed to pieces, but they found you still alive. Took you to a hospital in London to patch you up, then down to us. State you were in, love; still had bruises like dinner plates – and cry – I never heard anything like it. You could have screamed for England, I can tell you. No one could get you to stop, except me. We just took to each other I suppose. Ended up I was the only one you would go to. Knew your own mind even then, you did. After a while I had this idea. I had a chat with Matron; real nice she was. Said it was against the rules as long as I worked at the orphanage, but things were still so bad, with people being bombed out of their houses, getting killed in the air raids or away fighting, that what rules there were no one took a lot of notice of.'

I can hear every word that she's saying, but they have no meaning. It's as if there's a dam between us and the words are building up like water on her side.

'Are you listening, Alice?'

I nod.

'D'you see what I'm saying, love? D'you understand?'

She waits for me to react. I don't.

'I had to leave, but that didn't matter. We were together. I came back to London after the war and tried to start a new life for both of us. Wasn't easy; money was short. I was near to my wits' end at times. But we were together and that's all that mattered.

'We struggled on for a few years until I met your dad. D'you remember that day? You were still only a little tot – about four – and animal mad! I had gone into the shop in Burdett Road; you stayed to stroke some old dog. When I came out there was this man talking to you. Think you were a bit scared, not used to men, but he seemed nice enough. I thought no more of it, but a few weeks later we were in the park, and blow me down, there he was again. He said it was fate. Like it was meant to be. We got chatting, one thing led to another . . .

'I thought it would be good for you to have a dad: someone you could look up to. Someone to look after you. I know things ain't that good between you and him at the moment, but it wasn't always like it, was it?'

Her face brightens.

'Here, d'you remember that time when he hid those pennies around the house, then made up the story about buried treasure? You were just a tot then. Really good story it was. Then he drew you that map and you had to find the treasure. Your face lit up when you found them pennies. It was a picture.'

The smile goes from her face and it's like it's going from inside her as well.

'I don't know why it all changed. Why did it all have to change?'

Her words trail off. There's a long silence. All I can hear is the ticking of a clock that I can't see. She tries to talk. Spaces get in the way of her words; words that don't want to be said.

'I never wanted to tell you any of this, love. I thought it would make our family . . . less real. Dad wasn't happy about that. He said that now the baby was coming you'd have to know that you weren't my real child . . .'

She looks at her hands, screws them together.

She stops. Words trail into silence. There are no words in the world to finish a sentence that starts like that. It's like someone has just stolen part of my life. Told me I'm not me any more. I'm a lie. I don't belong to anyone. I'm floundering in thoughts. Struggling with questions. 'But what about my dad – my real dad? And who is my real mum?'

Mum doesn't look at me. She's picking at the bed-clothes.

'I'm sorry, love. There's something else you have to know. When they found you in the ruins of that house there were no other survivors. Your mum . . .' She stops, stares at the limp curtains by the bed. 'Your real mum and dad must have been killed.'

I look around. I just want to get out. Suddenly the air is choking me. The walls are growing, towering over me. I'm a dot. A speck of dust in the room. The voices around me telescope into a whisper. Still the walls grow. Throbbing. Words drown me.

'. . . but I love you, I love you like you're my own flesh and blood. Don't you ever forget that. I'll always love you like you was my child.'

Everything stops. Nothing moves. The curtain sways and is still. The pounding in my ears stops. I look at my mum as if for the first time. Look at her but see someone who isn't my mum. I watch as two tears fill the edges of her eyes, then brim over.

I hear myself. I hear a voice I don't recognize as mine. A still, small voice.

'But I thought . . . I thought I *was* your child, Mum.'

I feel a hand on my shoulder. I know it's Mrs Gilbey.

'Are you all right, Alice?' she says quietly.

I can't talk. There's only one thing I can think of doing. She tries to stop me but can't. Nobody could. I push past her.

I'm running. Through the warren of corridors leading to more corridors. Through doors opening out on to more doors. Going on for ever. I don't know where I'm going. I don't care. I run like the wind. I run like an animal fleeing from a predator. Like in a nightmare. Running. Running to get away from danger. I hear Mum call me.

'Alice, wait. There's something else, something you've got to have. It's important. Alice, wait.'

But I'm waiting for no one.

# ★★★ 19 If ifs and ands were pots and pans

It drops through the letter box while I'm trying to eat some toast. Don't feel much like eating. An envelope with my name on it, but no stamp. I look at it. Feel . . . I can't really explain how I feel any more. It's like another life is growing around me, covering up the life I had. I'm the butterfly going back into the chrysalis. Everything seems the wrong way round.

I put the toast down. Pick up the envelope. I recognize Mrs Gilbey's handwriting straight away. I glance up at the old clock. Quickly start to put on my coat as I make my way out. I mustn't be late for school again. Try to eat my toast while putting my coat on. Not one of my best ideas. Get margarine everywhere.

I start to read the note walking along. Not even a note really, just a few scribbled lines saying how there's something inside the envelope that Mum had wanted to give to me the other day. I start to feel nervous, my fingers tremble. It's like the story my mum was telling me still isn't over.

I shake the envelope. Something falls out into my hand. It's a bit of a photograph. Been torn in half. It's shadowy. Bit out of focus. Looks like a man holding a baby. One arm cradles the baby and the other seems to be going around someone's shoulder. A woman, I think, but whoever she is she's not in my half of the photo, so I can't tell for sure. I look back at the note, puzzled.

'. . . I know you were upset, Alice, but your mum was only doing what she thought was best. Try to remember that. Anyway, she thought it was also time you had this. Apparently it was found in that old biscuit tin of yours. Remarkable, isn't it? It was right by you when they found you.

'The photo looks like it's been taken in a garden; you can see some trees and the house in the background. It's a bit gloomy though, I had to get my magnifying glass. Your mum said they thought the baby must be you, so maybe the man holding you is your real dad. Wish we had the other half; that would make things a bit clearer. Your mum says no one knows who took it or how it got torn or where the other half of it is. Strange it was left in your old tin though.'

I look at the face of the little girl. She doesn't look much like me, but then babies change. Grow up. She's got a fat face, a little bonnet falls half over it. It makes me smile.

Mrs Gilbey's right. It is a garden and there are trees: that's what's making the photo dark. Casting shadows. I try to see who it is who's holding me. A ragged tear rips through the figure, but through the shadows I can just see the man's face. He's looking down at me and he's smiling.

For just a second I get that feeling; the feather touching my face feeling. Which is strange because as far as I know I'm not in trouble. I sigh. Put the photo back in my pocket for safety. Another problem I can't solve. Another mystery I'll never get to the bottom of. I make my way to school.

I'm trying to concentrate on the writing on the board, but I can't. The numbers jumble themselves up before my eyes. I try to do the sums but my thoughts scatter. Miss Lacey comes up to me in class and whispers in my ear. Sister Vincent wants to see me. She's never asked to see me before. I think she must know.

I make my way out of the classroom, feeling as if everybody is looking at me. As if they all know that I'm adopted. That I have no real mum or dad. I go down the stairs and into the corridor. Her room is on the left-hand side, just before the door that leads to the playground. The door is half open. I knock.

'Come in.'

It's a cross between a big cupboard and a small room. Untidy. Stacks of papers, piles of plimsolls, paperweights and potted plants. A filing cabinet is shoehorned into a corner. There's no window. A light is on.

Sister Vincent is tall. Fills the room. She's writing with a fountain pen. She has a kind face. Looks up as if she has forgotten who I am, or why she sent for me. She stops writing and carefully puts the top on the pen. That's the way I would do it if I had a fountain pen – thoughtfully, as if I were screwing up wonderful ideas. Storing them in the pen case until I'm next ready to use them.

She shuffles the papers together. 'Ah, Alice, come in.' She points to the chair.'

She looks unsure. Waits until I'm sitting down. Then says, 'I had a lady in to see me yesterday, a Mrs Gilbey. She lives quite close to you, I believe.'

She stops, as if giving me a space to say something, like I *should* say something, but I'm learning not to fill those spaces.

'She tells me things have been difficult for you for a while now.' She reads the look in my eyes, 'It's all right, Alice. She wouldn't say exactly what the problem was . . . ' She gives a little, uncertain smile. It plays around the corners of her mouth. Cat and mouse.

It dawns on me why I'm here. She wants me to tell her myself. She is nice and kind, but I don't want to say anything to her. Not here. Not now. In some ways I wish I could.

' . . . I just thought maybe you . . . '

I stay silent. Mouse escapes. Cat vexed.

'It's important that we know these things, you know. If there are problems at home . . . '

Relents.

'Anyway, I know your mother is in hospital and Mrs Gilbey was worried that you would be . . . ' again the pause ' . . . all right?'

'I'll be fine, Sister.'

'Are you sure, my dear?'

I'm not really sure if I'm sure of anything any more. I look at my feet. Funny how you do that when you don't know what to say. Look at your feet, as if they know something you don't.

Sister Vincent waits. I shuffle. She gives a long sigh. 'Ah, well. So be it. You are in our prayers. I thought you should know that.'

'Thank you, Sister.'

I breathe a sigh of relief. Be glad to get out.

'God bless you, child. How is your mother, by the way?'

I want to say, 'I don't know who my mother is, Sister.' I say, 'Fine, thank you.'

She turns back to her papers. Picks up her pen. Just as I'm about to leave she says, 'Sister Bernadette tells me that your play is going well.'

'Thank you, Sister.'

'It's an interesting story.' She smiles. 'Very interesting. Where did you get the idea from?'

'I don't know, Sister.' Never really thought about it before.

'Off you go then, Alice. We'll remember you all in our prayers.'

When the bell goes for the end of the day I walk out into the front playground. Summer's a tease. Hot one minute, cold the next. A grey sky falls on me. Sits half an inch above my head, pressing down, squashing out the light.

I walk home not really noticing anything. My feelings are so mixed up. I still love my mum, but she isn't my mum. Does that make any difference? I have half a photograph and half a life. I'm a bit scared, but deep down I know I have to find out what's going on. Why is it that Reggie turns up and all this stuff starts? If he is telling the truth, what's happening to the two of us and why?

The questions jumble in my head so that there's no room for anything else. I have no way of answering any of them. I don't even know where to start. Suddenly I'm almost home. I turn the corner.

Reggie's sitting on the pavement outside our flats. He sees me and waves. Flash is beside him, his chin resting on the ground.

I wave back. I wonder how long he's been sitting there. He gets up. Funny, me and Reggie. We seem to go round in circles, never quite touching each other. Musical-chairs friendship, with one chair and music that never stops. Round and round. Flash gets up, yawns and stretches; rolls over for a tickle.

Reggie smiles. 'C-coming out?'

I nod. Do my best to smile back. Best isn't good enough. My voice sounds hard. 'I am out.'

He looks hurt. 'Yes. S-silly question.'

I feel sorry. It's not his fault.

So, I say it. 'Sorry.'

'What f-for?'

'For what I said last time.'

'Yes, so am I.'

'What you sorry for?'

Gets his own back. 'For what you s-said last time.' He grins. 'Even if I can't remember what it was.'

'I called you a liar. Think I might have said bloody liar.'

'That's a double apology, then.'

'Don't push your luck, mate.'

He grins. I realize I'm hungry. 'I'll just get a piece of bread and jam. Want some?'

He nods.

I go in first: check that Bert isn't home. Then I let us both into the front room. It's damp and empty, as if no one has lived here for years. The room smells of old cooking. Plaster is peeling off the walls. I put on a light. It helps a bit. I open the cupboard. There's some bread there, stale but not mouldy.

'You all right?'

'Here, pass me that jam, will you? Crust OK?'

'Yeah, I like crusts. I s-said are you all right?'

'I heard you.'

I can feel him looking at me. I don't look at him. Then he reaches out. Touches my hand.

'It'll be all right s-soon, Alice.'

'You reckon?'

I pass him the crust.

Maybe I still need more time to get things right in my own head. I wonder if there's enough time in the world to do that.

The jam is sweet. You can taste the strawberries. Reggie looks funny with his lips red from the jam. He tosses a bit to Flash, who wolfs his down in no time and stands looking up for more.

Reggie says, 'If you want t-to talk to me about things . . . ?'

'Thanks.'

The sun peeks out to see if anyone has noticed it's been hiding. Should be ashamed of itself. We go out and just walk. Anywhere. Aimless. End up over near the bombed houses, where we had the bonfire. You can still see where it was. I kick fragments of charred wood like I expect to find something there. A bit of magic maybe.

There was a storm last week. Most of the canvas that we used as a roof over the air-raid shelter was ripped off. What's left flaps about like a bird trying to take off. The place feels sad. Most of the things we kept inside – the comics, a few games – are lying in damp piles.

We look around for the canvas. Don't find it. I check in my hiding place for the biscuit tin. It's still there. I touch the lid for luck. Peer at the picture of the little girl. Wish I was with her in that field with the faded blue sky overhead. Wonder again what that is on the ground near her. I try to see what's under the rust spots and cracked paint. I do that every time, as if one day it'll suddenly be clear.

'You all right?'

'What?'

'You keep s-staring at that tin.'

‘Yeah. Fine. Just wondering.’

‘What about?’

‘Nothing.’

I put it back. Pick up bits and pieces of our things – I don’t know why – like I’m trying to put something back together again that won’t go.

Reggie takes out his knife, picks up a piece of wood and starts to cut slivers from it. The wood shavings make patterns on the ground. Curls of white wood against the black earth, like writing. He cuts down hard. Pulls the knife through the wood, slicing it in two. Then he picks up the large piece and begins to sharpen it to a point. He uses the wood like a dart, throwing it into the ground.

Flash thinks it’s a game, seizes his opportunity, grabs it and runs off, shaking it like a rat.

Then, for some reason, I make up my mind. ‘Reggie?’

I hear in my voice that I’m going to tell him. He looks up.

‘Something happened the other night. It might have just been a nightmare but . . . ’

I tell him about the snake-belt, but even as I’m doing it things get mixed up in my head. I was asleep. I woke up. I know Bert hit me: I had the marks to prove it, but what about the other stuff?

Did I really make him see what I was seeing, or was it just my imagination working overtime? Maybe I only dreamed that part. Veronica told me once that when you’re sleeping you sometimes make things happen in your dreams that you wished had happened in real life.

Reggie doesn't say anything for a while. We just walk.

'I know you're confused about things, Alice, b-but it's like I told you. You're f-finding out about yourself now. Soon you'll know. Until then we have to stick together. That way we'll be stronger.'

'But what do I have to do?'

'B-believe in yourself. Believe that you can do anything.' He pauses. 'What about your stepdad? What did he say about what happened?'

'Nothing. He's hardly home now but . . . '

'But what?'

'I get the feeling that he's always around.'

'What d'you m-mean?'

'Can't explain, just like wherever I am he's there too, watching me. Like he knows . . . '

'Knows what?'

'I don't know. Blimey, I'm beginning to sound as barmy as you do.'

We walk and walk. Don't say much. Wrapped up in our thoughts. Together. On our own. By the time we get back the sun's starting to slide down a dusty-red sky. We cross the bomb site, walk along Sidney Street towards Watney Street.

The market's still open. Stall lights beginning to glimmer on. The stallholders are busy, selling fruit and vegetables. Oranges tumble on a spiky green cloth doing its best to look like grass. Apples and pears are piled high into polished pyramids; I'd love to take the bottom one away and watch all the others fall, but I don't. There are some clothes stalls too. Heaps of clothes piled high. Women toss them about, looking for bargains that aren't there.

We wander in and out of the darkness, sometimes stopping under the bright bare bulbs of the stalls, sometimes standing in the shadows just watching people. Reggie stops to talk to a man on a stall who's bent down to stroke Flash. The light shines off the man's bald head. He straightens. Tells Reggie he used to have a dog just like Flash once. Best friend he ever had. He polishes an apple on the leather apron he's wearing and gives it to Reggie. Sees me and gives him another. I'm still hungry and bite into mine. Juice spurts out, sharp and delicious. Hurts my teeth. Flash is nosing among the last piles of rubbish, crawling underneath stalls and getting in everybody's way. Reggie puts the piece of string back around his neck and we walk on.

We're on the edge of the market now. We cross Commercial Road and go into Sidney Street, Flash pulling at his lead trying to chase shadows. I look over my shoulder. Get a feeling that someone is watching us. I shiver. There's no one there. Just the dark.

'There's something else I want to tell you.' It comes out before I can stop it. I don't really mean to tell him, but I suppose it's been building up in me. The words Mum spoke in the hospital growing, getting bigger and bigger in my head.

'I went to see my mum in hospital last week. She told me something.' I stop. I can't say it at first. To say it makes it real. Then I force the words out. Traitor words. 'She told me . . . ' I take a breath. 'I'm adopted. I'm not her real child.'

There. Not so difficult after all. The words sound so simple I can't believe I've just told him something so important to me. That's the thing with words. They're there day after day. Doing what they're told. Obeying instructions. Open your mouth and out they come. Soldiers of information. Never a second thought. Never question an order. Then one day it's your feelings they have to explain. Describe what can't be described. Down goes a soldier. Shot through the heart.

I look at Reggie. He stares straight ahead; looks really sad. Takes off his glasses. Quickly wipes them on his sleeve. I carefully take out the photograph.

'She gave me this. Well, she gave it to Mrs Gilbey to give to me. It's a photograph. It's me as a baby. It's got torn. See? I'm being held by a man and there's someone else, looks like he's got his arm around her. Trouble is, that's the missing bit.'

I'm not looking at Reggie's face but I can feel him change. Hear it in his voice.

'Here, let me see.'

He holds out his hand. I was right. There's a look in his eyes. He takes the photograph. He stares at it for ages. I get the feeling he wants to say something, but he looks as if he can't believe what he's seeing. He turns it over. Then back. Peers at it again.

'Reggie? You all right?'

There's a long pause. I wonder if he's ever going to say anything. Then he does.

'This is it, Alice, part of the p-puzzle. Part of the story. It's all s-starting to make sense at l-last. There's s-something I can show you now.'

'Well, go on then, if you've got something that's going to make any sense of all this you'd better show me.'

'I can't, not yet. I just need to be sure. To check something.'

'Here we go again.'

'No, I p-promise as soon as I'm sure I'll show you. Can I k-keep this for a while?'

'Suppose so. Keep it safe though. It's the only photo I've got of me as a little kid.'

He smiles. 'I'll guard it with my life then.'

We reach the corner where Sidney Street turns left into Hawkins Street. Muffled light seeps from curtained windows. Street lights struggle, glimmer yellow. One lamppost wears a bicycle-tyre necklace. Ropes dangle from another one where kids have been playing swings.

Norman's dad is putting a nosebag on Daisy. She's usually kept in the yard where he works. He only leaves her outside his house when he wants to get an early start. She chomps hungrily. Shuffles her feet. The metal on her hooves rings out like bells.

We're partly walking and thinking and partly walking and talking. 'Did your mum know anything else? I mean, how you got to the children's home, or anything about your real parents?'

'No, she thought they must have been killed in the bombing raid. Funny, it all feels so mad. One day I was Alice Makin, now I don't know who I am. That's pretty scary. Not to know who you are or where you come from.'

'You do know who you are, Alice. You're you. Nobody can ever take that away. It doesn't m-matter who your mum and dad are, what m-matters is what you are . . . in your heart. You're a special person.'

Why did he have to go and say that?

I stop. Get out my handkerchief.

'You all right?'

'Just got something in my eye.'

'You know your m-mum loves you. That's the important thing.'

'Oh yeah? And what about my real mum?'

'I'm sure she loves you as well, Alice.'

Suddenly I'm crying. It's not like me – usually I keep it all bottled up; Little Miss Tough Guy. That's what you have to do around here to survive. Don't let 'em see you care. Keep it all in. But I do care. That's the point. Maybe that's the problem.

Reggie puts his arms around my shoulders. Drops Flash's string. Even Flash seems to know something's wrong: he licks my hand, then nudges me with his nose.

I shiver. The air changes. It's suddenly cold. I feel the darkness like I did that night in my bedroom. Like you could reach out and touch it. Thick. Heavy. In the wedge of shadow that angles out from the wall, something moves. I stop. Wipe my eyes.

'You all r-right?'

'Not sure. There's something over there.'

Flash growls. It moves from the shadows. A cat. Black, except for a white tip on its tail, flicking about in the darkness. It's watching us. But it's the eyes that make me catch my breath. Cold eyes that stare straight into mine. Like it's looking inside me. Like it knows me, really knows me. Flash moves towards it. I bend down to try and grab the string – too late. The cat hisses. A spiteful, vicious hiss. Flash barks loudly, then flies off like an arrow from a bow. Reggie yells. The cat turns and waits for Flash, waits like it's laying a trap. Then it runs.

I don't really see what happens next. It rushes across the road in a blur, heading for Mr Higginbottom's milk cart. Flash follows. This is his territory and no strange cat is going to outsmart him!

The cat dodges in and out of the shadows. Cloaks itself in the darkness. Weaves in and out of the night. Torments Flash.

I hear Reggie's voice call, 'Flash, here boy. Come on, Flash!'

Flash hesitates for a second: looks back at us, then at the cat. He barks once as if to let us know he won't be long, unfinished business, then takes off, barking loudly at the shadows. The two of them are a rushing blur. Flash catches up with the cat just as it's about to reach Daisy's feet. At the last minute the cat turns and looks back at Flash, then it springs through the air towards Daisy, its claws unsheathed. It buries them in the horse's back. Daisy snorts in pain. Stamps angrily. Tries to shake off what was on her back. But the cat has already gone. Vanished in the shadows. Melted into thin air.

Flash arrives in a bundle of fur. Chasing nothing now. Sees Daisy. Tries to stop. He's going too fast. He cannons into her legs. Daisy tosses her head violently. I stand there. It's as if this moment is going to last for ever. Me and Reggie looking across the road at Flash. Fixed in time. Frozen here. Watching. Waiting. Flash is right under Daisy's feet. Trying to get out. But he's trapped there. She shakes herself, snorts furiously, then kicks out with her back legs. Reggie shouts, but it's all like a bad dream now. I hear a terrible howl. A thud. Then silence.

All I want in the whole world at that moment is for Flash to run back to us. I call out. Hold my breath. Will him to come back. Against the light of a distant window something catches my eye. Someone is standing there. A trail of cigarette smoke rises into the air. Sparks fly as the glowing end flicks through the air.

# ★★★ 20 Flash

I'm aware of a light going on in Mr Higginbottom's window. Reggie runs past. Something takes over, making me move, but my body seems heavy. It takes me ages to get across the road. By the time I reach the shadows of the cart Norman's dad is coming out of his front door, silhouetted against the light. He's shouting something about how he's going to 'kill those bloody kids'. For a moment I can't see Reggie and then I almost fall over him. A shaft of light picks him out. He's kneeling, hunched in the darkness. His head bowed, holding a small bundle in his arms. A small bundle of black and white fur. I look up to see Mr Higginbottom.

'What the hell . . . ?' He stops, calls back into his house. 'Ellen, fetch a blanket. Hurry up.'

Reggie looks up at me. I can see his face clearly in the oblong of light coming from the open door. It has no expression. The sticking plaster has come off his glasses. From the pavement a small pool of blood drips slowly into the gutter. He says in a voice I can hardly hear, 'Get Granddad, Alice. Get Granddad.'

I feel nothing except my heart pounding as I run up the

stairs and bang at the door. Somewhere a baby cries. A man shouts. The door opens, and a chink of light escapes on to the landing.

'Granddad, quick. Come quick.'

'What is it, lassie?'

'You've got to hurry. Something's . . . Flash . . . oh, please, come on.' I hear words stumbling out of my mouth. Mixed up in the wrong order.

Granddad hobbles down the creaking stairs after me. He seems slow. Old. The light on the stairs is out. I go down first and stay close to him, in case he falls. If he does I hope he falls on me, that I'm knocked unconscious. Then, when I wake up, this will all be over, like some nightmare that never happened.

We go quickly into the chill of the night. Mr Higginbottom has brought a torch. Its weak yellow beam pokes its finger into the darkness. Reggie is sitting as I left him, cradling Flash. Someone has put a blanket around his shoulders.

It seems to take Granddad a while to work out what's happened. As if he can't believe what he's seeing. Very gently he bends over Reggie. Carefully, as though he is touching something too delicate and valuable to be touched, he lays his hand on Flash. He says nothing for a while, then he puts his arm around Reggie's shoulders.

Mrs Higginbottom comes out of her house carrying a tray of hot tea. It steams in the darkness. Her husband lights her path like an usherette in the cinema.

Norman follows her, in pyjamas and wellington boots with his rifle over his shoulder. He kneels down and puts his arm around Reggie. In the darkness the two figures merge into one. Almost as if Norman has turned into a blanket and has draped himself over Reggie.

Mrs Higginbottom puts the tray down on the pavement. 'Drink this, Reg.'

I've never heard anyone call him Reg before. Reggie doesn't move. Mr Higginbottom offers a cup to Granddad. He smiles his thanks, but shakes his head. I do the same.

After a while Granddad eases his arm under Flash's head. 'I'll take him for a minute.'

Reggie looks up at him as if he doesn't recognize him. His mouth opens. No words come out.

Granddad says, 'We need to get him home, son.' Then adds, 'Into the warm, eh? Let's get the poor fellow into the warm.'

Slowly, as if he can't bear to release his grip, Reggie moves his arm, lets his dog go. Carefully Granddad cradles the dark shape. Stands up.

Reggie says, 'Wait.'

He takes the blanket off his shoulders and wraps it round Flash. Then he gets up, turns and looks at me. 'It'll be all right, Alice. I p-promise.'

And all I can think is that after all this he's still thinking of me. Suddenly I don't care about what's happening to me. All I want is for Flash to be all right.

'I won't be a minute. I'll nip home and leave a note. I'll come up.'

They don't seem to hear me. They're concentrating on the bundle. Moving slowly. Gently.

In our front room, which is really the back room, I switch on the light. I find the box of matches in the drawer, strike one and light the greasy, dirty old gas cooker that stands in the corner. This, I know, will warm up the room quickly.

I sit down at the table. The bread is still out, with the jam, where I left it. If only we could go back. If only. I push the loaf to one side and put my head on the table, realizing for the first time how tired I am. A single tear trickles down my cheek and into the corner of my mouth. It tastes salty.

More tears follow. I try to think them away. *Maybe we should get the roof on our camp fixed. Get some really strong canvas.* My face is wet. *Keep out the rain and the cold. Take a torch over there.* Tears drip. I smear them away. Pretend I'm not crying. Think good thoughts. *It's my birthday soon. Maybe I can get a torch then, and some comics. Make it really snug. Yes, that will be good.*

But suddenly my body is shaking. I hear myself sobbing. Crying as though I will never stop again. As if there is nothing left in the world now except tears. The tears stream down my face. On to my arms. Fall in blotches on to the table. A flood of emptiness washes over me. Takes my breath away. Chokes me. Fills me. And I cry. And I cry.

I cry for Flash. I cry for Reggie. I cry for myself. I cry for everybody.

# ★★★ 21 Flowers

I get up from the table. Fill the tin bowl with cold water and wash my face. The chilled water sucks out my breath. Refreshing. It wakes me. I look quickly in the mirror. Red eyes stare back.

I climb the stairs to Reggie's. Knock in a whisper. Hold my breath.

The door opens. Granddad smiles. He seems pleased to see me. Steps aside. 'Hello, Alice. Come on in.'

Flash is lying on the settee, the blanket still around him. Reggie crouches by his side, one arm around his dog. Flash lies quite still. On the floor is a blood-soaked strip of cloth. Looks like it's been torn off a sheet. The bare bulb in the ceiling gives off hardly enough light to disturb the gloom.

I don't know what to say, so I don't say anything. I crouch alongside Reggie, put my arm around him. He looks at me. He feels cold.

'Will he be all right?'

Flash stirs. Grumbles.

'Your voice, he knows it's you . . . I don't know. It's a bad injury. We can't move him.'

I feel better. If he can recognize my voice . . . I leave the thought unfinished. I reach out slowly, put my hand on Flash. He doesn't move. It's like he's asleep, the way I've seen him so many times before. Dreaming. Twitching at other dogs, chasing the ghosts of cats – just dreaming.

Light drifts in lazily. The sun blinks in through the curtains. Space yawns yellow.

The knock wakes me. I open my eyes slowly. Granddad is asleep in the chair, head back, mouth open. Gurgling out a thin snore. Reggie is stretched out on the floor, one hand reaching up. Keeping in contact with his dog. Refusing to let go, even in sleep. Flash is cocooned in the blanket, the tip of his nose sticking out. I go to the door.

Norman stands there. A tin helmet on his head. A bunch of daisies and thistles in a rolled-up piece of newspaper in his hands.

'All right?'

'Not bad. Like your helmet.'

'Thanks. I made it. One of my mum's old saucepans.'

'Right. Looks . . . er . . . nice.'

He seems disappointed. 'Nice?'

I backtrack. 'Well . . . ' Can't think what to say. 'Not nice?'

He puts me out of my misery this time. 'Brought these.' He hands me the bunch of daisies and thistles.

'Right.'

He sees my look. 'For Flash.'

''Course. I don't think you can give dogs flowers, Norm.'

He seems puzzled. 'They're weeds.'

''Course. Silly me.'

'Our goats eat 'em all the time.'

I see the connection. 'Right. Thanks.'

'How is he?'

'Don't really know. I only just woke up. Reggie's asleep.'

'Maybe I can come back later and see him?'

'Sure.'

He turns. 'Don't forget to give him the weeds.'

'No. I won't.'

I turn back into the room. It's so still. Nothing moves. It's like I'm looking into a painting. I tiptoe over to the couch. Carefully move Reggie's hand. He mumbles and goes back to sleep.

I want to be the one to keep watch. If it's good news, I'll be the first to tell him. If it's not, I don't want him to be the first to find out. I push the thought away. Reach out and slowly move the blanket away from Flash.

# ★★★ 22 Talking

I'm about to climb over the banisters, but I stop myself. I don't need to do that now.

I've been dreading seeing Reggie. Putting it off. I just don't know what to say. I saw Granddad in the street yesterday. He came up to me. Took hold of my hand. Told me that they took Flash to Swan Island, rowed out and buried him there. Reggie thought Flash would like that.

I knock gently. It seems strangely quiet. After a while the door opens.

Granddad smiles. 'Good to see you, Alice. Reggie shouldn't be gone too long. Come in for a while?'

'Thanks.'

The room is cosy and warm. It smells of sleep and cooking. There's an old settee, shedding horsehair. A brown armchair with two patches worn away where Granddad rests his elbows. A big wardrobe like the one Mum wants. It has patterns spreading out in the wood like they've been painted on, except no artist would have been good enough to have painted like that.

He looks at me.

'How are you?'

He's asking a question but it's as if he knows the answer.

Under the window is a piano, black as polished coal. It looks somehow powerful. Gold patterns twist in the wood like lace. It shines, reflecting the light. I go up to it. Touch it.

'I'm all right. What about Reggie?'

He shakes his head,

'He's taking it badly. After you, that dog was his best friend.'

I think about the two of them. Always together.

'Things have been a bit rough for you too, lass. So much happening; so much to take on. Still, you'll come through it. Just like he did, like he will now.'

He stares into space. His eyes seem miles away. I sit at the piano. Open the lid. After a while he says, 'Can you play, Alice?'

I shake my head.

'Can you hold a tune?'

I touch the keys gently. Run my fingers up and down, looking for a pattern. I thought, stupidly, that I would just have to touch the keys and that would be it. Almost as if the piano would recognise me and could play itself through me. It's not like that. The keys are a black and white mystery. A confusion of noises waiting to make themselves heard.

'I don't know.'

He hums a tune I've never heard. 'Hum that back to me.' I do.

'You've a good ear all right. Look, just try these keys to begin with.'

He plays a Christmas carol. 'You have a go.'

I get stuck in the middle.

'Watch again, carefully.' He plays again. 'You have to have faith, Alice. Believe in yourself. Go on, have another go. '

I repeat it.

'Excellent. I think we'll make a pianist of you yet. Don't play much myself these days. It seems a shame that it doesn't get used. Move over a bit.'

He sits beside me and plays the carol properly. It sounds like a running river, like the sun in summer and the snow in winter. When he finishes, we both just sit there for a while in the silence.

'Will you show me how to play like that one day?'

He smiles. 'I think we might be able to manage that.'

I hear Reggie come up the stairs. Even recognize his footsteps now. He opens the door. Looks different. Grown up.

Granddad gets up. 'Ah, there you are. You've got a visitor.'

Reggie smiles. There's sadness in his eyes, but something else too. Something in the way he's looking at me. Like he knows something. It's as if now there's some strong force between us. Tying us together, now and always.

We cross the bridge over the canal and go down the steps on to the towpath. I like it here. Not many people. A world inside the world. It's quiet. The sun sleeps in the sky, tucked up in its blanket of cloud. A soft breeze barely whispers; even the wind is holding its breath. It seems strange without Flash. I keep expecting to look around and see him. Sometimes Reggie stops. Waits, like he's forgotten he's gone.

The canal runs parallel to the back of our school. You can see it from the playground. Often there are barges making their way to the docks or the wharves. Today there's nothing. The water ripples gently. Distorts images. Shimmers reflections. We sit on the low wall. Moss spills out of the brickwork, damp and green. I pick bits off, Reggie does the same.

A pale sunbeam dips its light in the water and winks. It's like neither of us want to talk but I guess sooner or later someone has to.

'I'm really sorry about Flash.'

'Yeah.'

'It was so unlucky. That horrible cat appearing from nowhere, then vanishing like it had never been there at all.'

Reggie looks at me. 'It wasn't just unlucky.'

'What d'you mean?'

'Don't you think it was all a b-bit too much of a coincidence, Flash, the cat, Daisy . . . '

I say it at last.

'You think my stepdad's behind all this, don't you? You have from the start. You think he's the one who's been trying to scare us?'

Reggie looks away from me. 'I've never trusted him. He's out to get us, Alice. I know he is.'

'But why? Why would he do that?'

'To show us what he can do, that he's more powerful than we are.'

'I just don't understand all this. It all sounds mad. It just doesn't make sense. Nothing does, any more. Sometimes I think I'm just imagining everything. That's it's all a bad dream and I'll wake up.'

'It's real all right. What he d-did to Flash was real enough. That's how I know we're in danger.'

I reach out, take his hand. He fumbles for a handkerchief and blows his nose.

'Flash was a good d-dog.'

'The best. Remember that time he bit Gary Spicer on the bum?'

'It was Gary's own fault. He shouldn't have been t-trying to climb over that fence.'

I think about this. 'No. Mind you, it *was* his own fence he was climbing over.'

Reggie picks up a cardboard box from the ground. Throws it into the water. 'True. But Flash wasn't to kn-know that, was he?'

He picks up a stone. Throws it at the box bobbing on the water. Misses.

I don't want to think about my stepdad any more. I pick up a stone too. Throw it. Miss. 'No, s'pose not.'

He picks up another stone. 'Mind you, Flash n-never

did like the Spicers.' Takes more careful aim this time. Throws it. Misses again.

I do the same. 'No, I s'pose he'd have bitten him sooner or later. He had good taste, Flash. He knew who to bite.'

He smiles for the first time. 'It probably wasn't.'

'Wasn't what?'

'A good t-taste.'

It takes a while for the penny to drop. I laugh. 'See what you mean.'

He picks up a big stone. Throws it. It hits the box. I pick up another, but before I can throw it the box rolls over and sinks.

Reggie gets up and walks on. I watch him for a while as he moves down the towpath with his hands in his pockets, his head slightly bowed.

We walk under the bridge. He takes out a packet of Refreshers, breaks the tube. Finds a mauve one. Hands it to me.

A narrowboat glides out of the tunnel behind us, bright with reds, golds and greens. I can see the name in gold on the prow. Theresa. That's my favourite name. A good sign. It moves through the water, engine purring, spluttering dribbles of water from the bilges.

'Oh, I almost forget to tell you. G-Granddad is taking Mrs Gilbey to the pictures on Saturday. I think they like each other.'

'That'll be good.'

He nods. He doesn't look at me, but in my mind's eye

I can see exactly the kind of look he has on his face.

'I only hope she remembers to fetch some money.'

The boat passes. Coughs black smoke from the red and black funnel. A woman appears on deck. She's carrying a baby in her arms. She has a short, fair ponytail tied back with an elastic band. She smiles, showing off a gap between her two front teeth. Girlish. Like her mouth has stayed twelve years old. She waves with one hand. Turns the baby towards us. It reminds me.

'Remember you said you had something to show me? Something to do with that old photo. A surprise.'

'The one with your funny h-hat on? Well, half on.'

'I think I look really cute.'

'Mmm, you did, what h-happened?'

'Shut your face. Well? When you going to show me?'

He looks thoughtful. 'It's your birthday s-soon, isn't it?'

'Couple of weeks. It's on a Saturday.'

'Good, that'll be a g-good time. I'll show it to you then. Make it into a little bit of a birthday p-present. I think it might help to explain what's going on.'

'How d'you mean?'

'You'll h-have to wait and see.'

'This present.'

'Mmmm.'

'Give me a clue.'

'Ask Sherlock Holmes. See if he can f-figure it out.'

'Spoilsport.'

I start scuffing the toes of my shoes on the ground – I

do that sometimes when I'm thinking – and I start to see little pictures in my head, of the times we've been together, the things Reggie has said. Funny how things that seem so stupid one day can startto make sense the next. I don't want to admit he's right, even to myself, but there's something in me that wants to believe him. I mean, what if there really is something called mind-touching and I can do it. It would be like making all the stories I've thought about come true.

'Oh well, if you're right about this mind-touching, the next few weeks could be . . . interesting.'

'It'll be that, all right. Just remember; we have to be on our guard. Together.'

I look at Reggie and know I want to be an Indian. I want to believe him. I want my mind to fly like a bird in the bright blue sky. I want to ride my imagination like a wild bucking bronco. What's wrong with a bit of magic?

'Hey, look. The sun's comin' out.'

# ⋆⋆⋆ 23 A fair time

I get myself ready for school. Have a quick wash. Spread some jam on a crust. I haven't seen Bert for days now, only a humped shape under blankets in the bedroom sometimes when I come home. There's a knock at the door.

'It's only m-me.'

'Hold on a minute.'

I open the door. Catch sight of myself in the mirror. Look a wreck. Reggie walks in. Sits on the table.

'You look t-terrible.'

'Thanks. I was just thinking how nice I looked.'

'Yes, that's what I meant to s-say.'

'Creep.'

'Granddad said if you want to, you can c-come and have your d-dinner with us tonight.'

'Double creep.'

'No, he d-did. Honest.'

'Thanks. But I'll have to check Bert's not home. You comin' to school, then?'

'Not today. There's s-something I've got to do.'

'You can't just keep bunking off whenever you feel like it.'

'Why not?'

''Cos you can't. You've got to go to school.'

'Why?'

'To learn things.'

'W-why?'

'I don't know. Stop asking stupid questions. So you can get a good job. Anyway, what d'you want?'

'I've just been over to Watney Street, there's a fair there. Fancy c-coming tonight?'

'I dunno.'

'Come on, we both n-need cheering up. We can just forget about things for a while.'

'Well . . . '

'Go on, it'll be good.'

Part of me wants to go and part doesn't. He smiles, a wide smile like a tin of beans opening. I get my coat.

'I've gotta go. I'll be late for school.'

'We can go on the dodgems if you want.'

I can't help smiling. Sometimes talking to Reggie is like talking to a little boy. Other times it's not.

'All right.'

'I'll knock f-for you.'

'Best not. I'll meet you in the passage about six.'

'Cor, is that the t-time?

'What about it?'

'Just thinking, you'd better hurry up or you'll be l-late.'

'Cheeky beggar.'

The day seems to linger. The hands of the clock in class

drag themselves round. I suppose the more I think about it, the more I'm looking forward to the fair. It seems ages since I've just done something ordinary. For the fun of it. Not thinking about anything else. That's the thing about a fair, there's so much going on you just lose yourself for a while.

When the bell finally goes I rush home. I start to clean up. Sweep the back yard. Seems to take ages. I do some work on the play. It's getting nearer and nearer. Trouble is, I'm getting stuck. Maybe it's all this stuff that's going on around me. I just can't seem to think of a good ending.

Then I get hungry. I spread some jam on a thick crust, and wolf it down. I look at the clock, go out into the passage. I'm just going to go up for Reggie when he comes down the stairs. He's got a grin on his face.

'Good, you're on t-time for once. Ready?'

'For anything.'

'Come on, then. Let's go.'

Outside, the twilight sky plots dusky seas. A lighthouse moon warns galleon clouds. Shipwrecks ahoy. We turn into Sidney Street and walk down towards Commercial Road to the fair. Caravans and lorries, tents and stalls, machinery and people. Mayhem. Noise. Fun. The lights glare, edging out the growing darkness. Coloured bulbs garland tents, merging into a warm haze of colour. Sounds ripple, music rolls like waves. We stop to take it all in. Listen to the magic.

'What's that noise?'

'It's the merry-go-round. I think its proper name is a carousel.'

Reggie thinks for a while. 'Merry-go-round is better.'

'Yeah.'

The sound drifts towards us. Draws us like a magnet. Stallholders call. Men and women laugh. Children shout. Bright lights scald the darkness, sandpapering our eyes. 'You got any money?'

He digs in his pocket. 'Not a l-lot.' Pulls out some coins. 'What about you?'

'One and six. Share?'

He nods. We walk into another world. Dodgems and merry-go-rounds, helter-skelters and ghost trains. Technicolour toys waiting to be captured on hoopla stalls. Goldfish in plastic bags, longing for new homes.

'Want s-some chestnuts?'

'Yeah!'

In the far corner a tin drum glows red as blood, shooting sparks into the black night. An old man hunches, warming his hands – part of the darkness, torn out of the shadows. The smell draws us on. On top of the drum, roasting chestnuts sigh in the heat. Reggie hands over a threepenny bit. The man squints at it, coughs loudly and scoops crackling nuts into a brown paper bag. We walk away examining our supper. Crispy, golden brown nuts.

My mouth waters. Reggie hands the bag to me. I take one and bite into the hot, sweet, salty flesh. It burns my tongue deliciously.

'Nice?'

'Great.'

Impatient, we toss the hot nuts from hand to hand like jugglers. Tumbling through crowds, twigs in a current.

'Look, dodgems over there.' Reggie gets squashed between women pushing prams overloaded with babies, men laughing, kids shouting.

'Where?'

He nods his head in the direction of the dodgems. 'Over there.'

We have to barge our way through. I get pushed, trip and land on a pram. A woman looks daggers at me. Reggie smirks.

'What you doing, playing pram dodgems?'

'Very funny. Just you wait.'

Eventually we disentangle ourselves from the crowd like threads from a jumper.

The man looking after the dodgems has long greasy hair. His sleeves are rolled up and he has a tattoo of a dragon on his arm. Reggie counts out some money and gets into a bright-red car. He has that cheeky look in his eyes and that little smile playing around the corners of his mouth that makes his lips twitch. He pushes at his glasses. 'You s-sure you want to do this? It can get a bit rough.'

'Don't you worry about me, this is war.'

We spend the next few minutes racing around. Trying to bash each other. Getting bashed. The watching faces are a blur. The noise of people laughing, yelling, and bumping dodgems blocks out everything else. Suddenly the cars slow and come to a halt. I can hear the music again. I get out and sit on the side. My legs feel wobbly. I do up my shoelace. Reggie gets out of his. Sits by me. I feel a hand on my back.

'Gotcha! Surrender or die.'

We both turn at once. The face is hidden by a black balaclava. Only the eyes show.

'Wish you'd stop doing that, Norman.'

He's chewing a bar of nougat. 'I could've slit both your throats.'

'Yeah, that nougat looks really dangerous.'

He pulls out a long knife. Black handle, floppy silver blade. Sharp as rubber. 'Liberated this off a German officer.'

'Put it away, Norm, before you rub yourself out.'

He drags the balaclava off his head. It rakes through his hair like a plough through fields. Underneath his face is red. His eyes shine.

'How long have you two been here?'

'Not l-long.'

'What you been on?'

'Couple of things. W-what about you?'

'Coconut shy.'

'Win?'

'No. I hit loads of them but they never came off the stands. I reckon they're glued on.' He chews on the nougat, pulling it out in long, tacky strands.

'You should watch out, Norman. That'll take your teeth out. You won't get into the army without teeth.'

'Wanna bit?'

We both shake our heads.

'I'm gonna go and win a goldfish. I ain't never had a pet.'

'What about your goats, Norman?'

'They ain't pets, my dad keeps them for their milk and that. Anyway, goats are stupid. Goldfish are clever.'

'Wh-what makes you think that, Norman?'

'That's obvious, mate, they can swim, can't they? Gotta go. See you later. And don't forget: take no pensioners.'

'Prisoners, Norm.'

'Yeah, them neither.' He sneaks off into the shadows. The nougat bar becomes a pistol. He massacres the crowd. Then a stray bullet spins him to the ground. He dies in agony. Again.

'That's twice he's been killed this week.'

'M-maybe his mum will knit him a medal.'

The crowds grow. Two rivers flowing from different directions. A torrent of people that meets in a narrow path between the coconut shies and the slot machines, then spills over. A monster flood. Full of people, all shapes, all sizes. Sticky with candy floss. Pink-mouthed, strawberry-iced. Beery-breathed. Swirling. Twisting. Not quite here. Not quite there. Not quite anywhere. Ladies in bright floral dresses. Kids red-eyed. I lose sight of Reggie. More lights glimmer in the darkness. More stalls spring up, opening their welcoming arms. Shadows spill into light. Light into shadows.

'Alice? W-where are you?'

A man steps forward from behind a stall. Shouts out a challenge to the crowd.

'Come on, test your strength. Make the bell ring. Show your sweetheart what a man you are.'

'I'm here, where are you?'

An old woman knocks into me. Nut-brown. Red scarf tied around her head. 'Lucky heather. 'Ere you are, sweetheart. Penny a bunch. Genuine lucky gypsy heather.'

And another, 'Read your fortune, handsome?'

'Penny a bunch, lucky heather.'

'Over h-here.'

'I can't see you.'

Plastic ducks bob on water jets. Sitting targets. Air rifles crack. Ducks stop bobbing. Float upside down. Dead as ducks.

Disembodied voices. Arguments and laughter. Singing out of tune.

Wish I had stilts. Ah, now I see him. 'Reggie.'

He hears me. Smiles. Waves.Then I think I hear another voice. It whispers in the wind. Calls my name. Sounds like my stepdad. I shake my head. Must be the excitement.

I look around again for Reggie. The crowd seems to fill my eyes. My head swims. I feel sick. Faces press in around me, blocking out my space. In my face. Pushing. Shoving.

It's like there are just too many of them. Like they can't be real. I call out, 'Reggie.' I see him for an instant then, like a monster whale, the huge crowd opens its mouth and swallows him whole. Spits out his voice. 'A…l…i…c…e.'

I have to get out. Find a bit of space. I move away from the bright lights and into the darkness. The wind is suddenly colder. The warmth that you get from being close to so many other people has gone. I take some deep breaths. A cloud bites off a piece of the moon, spits it out as smoky white light. I keep walking. Probably best to get away, just in case he really is in the crowd.

The noise of the fair melts into the night like the candyfloss on my tongue. I pass the caravans, where the fairground people sleep. They're in darkness. Everybody is busy at the fair. The shadows get longer. Giants, changing with the lights. Sometimes following, stealthily silent. Sometimes in front, lying in wait. I move further into the darkness. The shadows disappear. Now only the humming buzzing of the generators keeps me company. Thick cables lie on the ground taking electricity to the fairground. There's a smell in the air. I don't trust the dark. Your mind can turn on you. Twist the ordinary out of shape. Silver moonlight slips from behind the clouds. In front of me a big striped tent hunches its shoulders. For a minute I can see the moon quite clearly, before it loses itself. Then I hear a sound: a thread of sound. A whisper. Like someone is calling my name. It sends shivers up my spine.

I decide to make my way towards the striped tent.

Maybe there'll be people around there. The moon dips in and out of clouds, weaves wispy trails of light. Tents press out from the night. The wind flaps at canvas, shusses out a whisper. A...l...i...c...e. Can that really just be the wind?

I start walking. Hear it again. A voice. Close by. He's here. He must be.

'Who's there, who is it?'

Nothing. Silence. One of the ropes holding the tent rattles back a laugh at me. The moon moves, casts off clouds, plunges into the dark ocean of the sky. It's light yellow, dull. From behind the caravans I hear a laugh. It's the way he used to laugh at my poems. Mock my stories. Not even a laugh really. Just a sound. A sound that meant I was no good. Rubbish.

I start to walk faster. The big top is just a few hundred yards away now. Shouldn't take long. I cast a quick glance behind. Footsteps. I freeze, straining my ears. Someone's breathing. I hear the voice again, louder this time.

'A...l...i...c...e'

A breath of sound. It frightens me.

'Reggie, is that you?'

I clutch at the straw of the question. Know the answer. The moon sinks. I can't see. Feel like I'm drowning in darkness.

'A...l...i...c...e.'

It's not Reggie's voice. I turn and walk quickly. The walk turns into a run. I'm trying to keep my eyes on the shadow of the big top. I'm running blindly now, shapes rise, tower over me for an instant then wreck themselves in the darkness.

The voice sighs out my name one more time. I try to run faster. I will my legs to pump harder. My breath rasps in my chest. I can sense someone is close by. Just as I turn my head something snags at my ankle. Flips me over into the night. I stumble. Sprawl in the mud. I lie still for a few seconds, not daring to look. My chest hurts. I can't catch my breath. Slowly I open my eyes. Turn around. Look up. Silence. Nothing. I sit up.

'A…l…i…c…e'

My blood chills. Sweat prickles.

The shadow slips out of the night. Moonlight sidles down. Sly. Cold. Lights up the space. I can hear breathing, a thin finger of sound.

'Who's there? What d'you want?'

My voice cracks. I try to get up. My legs are jelly. I want to scream, shout, run away, but I can't move. The air trembles. A shadow ripples across me. Something glitters in the threads of moonlight. Eyes watching me.

'Please . . .' I blink and he's there. Like he's been there all the time. Holding his belt. Weighing it in his hands. Tap-tapping it against his palm. I shut my eyes. I try to think of the snake, the way I beat him the last time. But it's like he's too strong. I haven't got enough energy. The breathing turns to a laugh. And all the time I can see him. Looking at me. Those terrible eyes.

My body tenses, waiting for the blow. I look around, desperate. Close by is a piece of wood. I inch my fingers towards it. If I can't fight him one way I'll just have to do it another.

I'm nearly there now. Just another fraction. My fingers are about to close on the wood.

A foot stamps down. Pins the wood to the ground. The shadow reaches out and grabs my shoulders.

My heart stops. I can't fight any more. I roll over and look up into the darkness.

'Gotcha. Surrender or die.'

It's Norman! It was Norman all the time. Relief turns to anger. 'Norm! You idiot, what you playing at.?'

'Sorry, Al, didn't mean to frighten you.

I feel sick. Start to get up. 'Well, you did. What d'you mean standing there like that, scaring the life out of me.'

He fidgets nervously, shuffles from foot to foot. 'Sorry, Al, I only know one way to stand.'

He pulls up his balaclava. 'You look terrible. You all right?'

'No thanks to you. Why'd'you do that?'

'What?'

'Follow me. Call out my name. Trip me. I could have killed myself.'

'I didn't! I was out on night patrol. I saw you running like someone was after you, then you tripped over the tent rope. I just came to see you're OK.'

I stare back into the darkness. Nothing moves. Silence.

'So, you wasn't following me?'

'No.'

'Did you see anyone around?'

'Like who?'

'Anyone? My stepdad? '

'No. Like I said, I saw you running but I couldn't work out why. You looked really scared though.'

I get up. Start to rub at the mud.

'Ain't seen Reggie about, I suppose?'

'Yeah, he was looking for you. He seemed really worried. Then I lost him in the crowd. So I thought I'd keep an eye open, make sure you were all right.'

'Thanks, Norm.'

'No problem. It can be a bit scary out here on your own.'

I take a deep breath, then feel something soft brush my face. Like everything's all right. There's nothing to worry about.

I look up. The moon dips in and out of clouds. It's all light and shadow, imagination and reality. Perhaps being an Indian has its drawbacks after all.

I shake myself. 'Come on, Norm, let's go and find Reggie.'

We dive back into the noisy crowds.

# ⋆⋆⋆ 24 Birthdays of a different kind

Today is Saturday. No school – and my birthday, all rolled into one. It's not going to be a usual birthday. Mum's still in hospital, so there won't be any presents, but I still feel good. There's something about a birthday when you don't have to go to school. Like that's your present. Freedom to do what you want. That's a present worth having.

I begin to think about all the things that have been happening. Wonder what Sherlock would make of it all. He'd probably go on about evidence again, as usual. Maybe this thing Reggie's going to show me will be the first real piece of evidence. The first piece. Maybe it will prove that mind-touching is real. And it will be obvious and we'll all stand around saying 'Elementary, my dear Watson'. Like the truth was staring us in the face all the time. I don't think.

I reckon he's found out something about that old photo. I asked Mrs Gilbey if she knew any more about it, but she said that all she knew was that it was found in my tin when I was a baby. I keep trying to guess what it can be. The questions whirlpool around in my head, round and round in smaller circles till they disappear down the plughole that's my brain.

I have a good wash at the kitchen sink and make myself tea and some toast. The grill is broken. The bread burns. I scrape off the black bits. Smother it with marge and crunch into it. Delicious. A birthday cake without any candles. I thought I might get a card from Mrs Gilbey, but I haven't. I feel a twinge of something, somewhere. She must have forgotten this year.

I'm hoping Reggie will knock. I wait and wait, pretending to myself that I've got things to do. Reasons not to go out. He doesn't come. The church clock in Sidney Street chimes out.

I decide to go up for him. Granddad's in, but he doesn't know where Reggie is. I tell him I'm going to the library and ask him to let Reggie know. He asks me to get him a book.

I take the long way up Commercial Road. Today I feel like seeing people, dodging traffic, soaking in the noise around me. So much has happened. So much has changed. The world is doing somersaults on a trampoline, holding my hand and taking me with it. It's scary and exciting at the same time. I almost believe the impossible is possible. Nonsense can sometimes make sense. That takes some thinking about. But now, in the busy, bustling street it seems that the only thing that matters is to be here. To be alive. To be thirteen. Happy birthday to me. I skip along like a little kid, singing to myself:

'Happy birthday to me,
Happy birthday to me,
Happy birthday, dear Alice,
Happy birthday to me.'

Rows of books 'shush' me with the sweep of the opening door. There's a place for singing and a place for not singing. I like it in the library. I can get lost in the books and forget about everything else for a while – blot it all out.

Mrs Bentley is the librarian. I like her because you know where you are with her. She's always the same. Her face is always the same. She always dresses the same. I wonder if she has a spare same face and several spare sets of the same clothes. She always has her hair in a bun with little bits straying on to her forehead. I sometimes think that they're always the same little bits of hair that stray, but I can't prove it. As I go in she smiles at me.

I walk along the aisles, touching books as if they're friends I'm visiting. Reminding them I'm here. It isn't warm or cosy like Mrs Gilbey's, but I feel safe here like I do at her house. I take a book from the shelf. Just pick one at random. It's old-looking, the cover scarred as if it's been in a battle. A faded red, with the letters of the title picked out in gold. I find a quiet corner up by the window. Sit on the floor and start to read.

When I open a book I usually lose myself in it, but

today isn't like any other day. Today is different. The book's only got half my attention. I keep hoping that Reggie is going to walk in through the door, or creep up and tap me on the shoulder. But gradually I lose myself in the pages, and the next time I look at the clock almost two hours have gone by.

Mrs Bentley smiles as she stamps my books, and says, 'Everything all right?'

I nod. Suddenly remember that I have to get that book for Granddad.

I find it and leave, opening the door slowly, still hoping that perhaps Reggie will be outside waiting for me. But there's no sign of him.

I walk back home. Doubts, nagging like a toothache, start to pull at me. Where is he? Why didn't he come to the library? He said he was going to tell me today. Why isn't he around?

I decide to go over to the camp. It starts to rain. Gentle rain, like it doesn't really want to make anyone wet. People push their umbrellas at the sky. Put their heads down.

I cross the bomb site. Suddenly I hear a noise coming from the air-raid shelter. It must be Reggie. My heart lifts. I can't wait to see him. I quicken my walk. Now I'll find out what's been going on.

## ★★★ 25 Passwords and parcels

But it's only the noise of canvas flapping against the walls. I sit and wait in the damp shelter for ages. Rain dances off the roof, splashes into puddles. It seems very empty here. The birthday feeling begins to wear off. I take slow walks to the places we go. The canal. Vicky Park. Hope I'm suddenly going to turn the corner and find him waiting there. See him walking towards me down the road. The wet streets are empty. I wander around. Feel like a stranger. Like I don't belong.

The day slips by. The gentle rain keeps falling. I watch the hours slowly pass. Time drip-dripping away with the rain. I watch it from shop doorways. From wet park benches. From empty alleyways. Chimed away by church bells. Waved away by people leaving friends. Lonely hours. I remember Mrs Gilbey saying that he and Granddad have moved around a lot, and I get a hollow feeling in my stomach.

I walk back to the flats. The street door is wide open. I walk down the passageway, my shoes leaving water footprints. My footsteps rebound from the walls. I manage a smile. I'm being followed by myself. I go to push open the door; it's ajar. My heart leaps. 'Reggie?' But the room is in darkness. I reach in for the light switch and . . . 'What?' For a second my knees actually buckle – my stomach drops. A hand shoots out from the darkness, grabs my wrist. I pull back and manage to click on the light switch.

'Well, well, look who's here?'

It's him. He must have been standing by the door in the dark just waiting for me. I try to pull free. His grip tightens, hurts my wrists.

He pulls me. I grab the door frame.

'Leave me alone.'

He bends down until his face is level with mine. Those cold grey eyes.

'Not so fast.'

Then he jerks back his arm and pulls me into the room. I stumble. Grab at a chair. It topples. I fall on to it. He's standing over me, looking down. He has a sneer on his face. He looks grubby like he hasn't washed or shaved for a while. I know he's been to the pub. His words slur like they're stones in his mouth. Something to be spat out.

'Reggie again, eh? Always Reggie with you. Reggie this. Reggie that. Wasting your time with him. You and him and your daft ideas. You should be here looking after me, keeping this place tidy. You think you're so clever. You and that bloody imagination of yours. Imagining you're something you're not, that's what you imagine.'

He starts to laugh. 'And you know what? It's all rubbish. Like the rubbish you keep in that sad old biscuit tin, the rubbish that you line up on the windowsill like it's something to be proud of and the rubbish in your head.

His voice changes. 'When you were a little girl it was different. You looked up to me then, but you had to go and get ideas, didn't you? Messing about with your writing and drawing. Thinking you were so special. Then that troublemaker upstairs came along.'

He takes out his tobacco tin. Tries to roll a cigarette. Drops most of the tobacco. He looks down at it as if he can't manage the effort to pick it up.

'Still, I should have known. You've always been ungrateful, selfish, full of yourself. You and your stupid made-up worlds. I should never have listened to your mother. I should have beaten it out of you years ago.'

I stand up. I'm nearly as tall as he is now. I look straight into his eyes.

'You're just a bully. I'm not scared of you any more.'

For a while he holds my stare.

'Oh no? Well, we'll see about that.'

Something flickers in his eyes. His mouth twists. His hands go to his belt buckle and I know what's coming.

'I forgot; it's your birthday today, isn't it? Well, maybe I should give you a little present of my own.'

He wraps the belt around his hands. The buckle is loose, flaps. I back away towards the door. Then I feel it again. The touch of a feather. A breath on my face. He stops. Looks around as if he'd felt something too.

'What was that?'

'What? I didn't hear anything.'

'Someone just said something.'

'I didn't hear anything.'

He looks at me, almost as it he's trying to make up his mind.

Then he shrugs. 'It'll keep.'

He does up his belt, pushes me out of the way, and slams out. I can hear him going down the passage.

I pick up the chair. Straighten the table. Why did he stop? He's never done that before. I pick up an envelope from the floor. It has my name on the front. It's in Mum's handwriting. It's only a bit torn. I take it back down the passage to my room.

I'm shivering. It's cold in here. Always is. But I'm not sure if that's why I'm shivering. I get into bed and pull the blanket over me. Her handwriting on the card is small and untidy. *Happy birthday, love, see you soon.*

I get out of bed and go over to the window for more light. I can see it better now. I put the card on the windowsill and curl up under the covers.

I wake with a jolt. Must have gone to sleep. Someone's tapping on the window. For an instant I'm frightened. Is it him? I get up. Swing my legs off the bed. Knock something off as I do so. I pick it up, trying to clear the sleep from my head. It's Granddad's book from the library. I go over to the window to see who's out there. But it's just the rain, patterning the glass.

I feel trapped. I have to get out from this cramped, damp little room. I'll take the book up to Granddad. Maybe Reggie will be there and I can find out why he's avoiding me. I go out into the dim passage. Creak up the stairs past the shadows. No games tonight. Knock hard. Knock again. No answer. Then I see it. A scrap of paper pinned to the door.

*Gone to Mrs Gilbey's*

I put it in my pocket, go back down the stairs and out into the street. Outside it's dark except for a thin line of light at the edge of the sky. The curtain of night, not yet pulled down far enough. It's still raining. Raindrops flurry like snow, layering my hair, battering the yellow light of the lamppost. Moths around a flame. Somewhere, far away, thunder drum-rolls. Faint glimmers of lightning pulse. I shudder.

I walk quickly, pulling my coat closer to my body. I'm looking forward to getting there. Thinking of the neat room. The smell of polish. I walk to the end of Hawkins Street. Turn right, into Lyndsay Street. Then down to number fourteen. Nearly there. Soon I'll see the light in the window that comes from the lamp which—

The disappointment stabs me like a pain. My thoughts

are cut off. There is no light in the window. The house is in darkness. My body shivers, fed up with being cold and hungry, with me always doing the wrong thing. My hand reaches out and knocks. Silence. I can't think what to do next. I feel beaten. Confused. There's no point standing here. I turn and begin to walk away, back up Lyndsay Street, thinking what a terrible birthday it's been.

'Alice.'

A soft voice. I look around. Can't see anybody.

'Alice.'

I see her white hair in the darkness, peering round the door. 'Emma, sorry, did I wake you?'

'No dear, I'm making myself a hot drink.' She looks up. 'Looks like a storm coming. You'd better not stand out there. Fancy joining me in some Ovaltine?'

'I would if I knew what it was.'

'Come on, then. You're a girl who doesn't mind taking a risk.' There's a tease in her voice. Then she says, 'It's like hot chocolate, but not. If you see what I mean.'

I laugh. Hot chocolate but not sounds good enough to me. As I get closer she puts on the hall light. Opens the door wider and lets me in. She shuts the door behind me. The light is bright. I blink, trying to get my eyes used to it. The hallway seems different, but it takes me a few seconds to work out why. Paper chains hang in arches from the wall. The kind that you make yourself from coloured pieces of paper.

Then the door to the front room opens. Someone

inside must have pulled it open. This is even stranger, since Mrs Gilbey lives alone, and at this moment is standing behind me.

'Go on, go through.'

I feel her hands on my shoulders, guiding me towards the door. The open doorway lets me see enough of the room to know that it, too, is in darkness.

Until I walk in. As I do, the light snaps on. The light is welcoming, comforting. There are even more paper chains, balloons as well. Over the fireplace is a big sign. It says:

HAPPY BIRTHDAY, ALICE

I blink, in case I'm dreaming. Sitting on the settee are Granddad and Reggie. A figure jumps from behind the door, a black balaclava hiding his face. Something sticks in my back.

'Gotcha! Hands up. Friend or foe?'

'Friend.'

'What's the password?'

'Dunno.'

''Ow d'you know that? Pass, friend. I would give you a kiss but I ain't got me gas mask on.'

I grab him and give him a kiss. That'll teach him!

Granddad gets up. 'Happy birthday, lassie. Come on in, you look cold.'

Reggie says, 'You took your time. I thought you were never going to come.'

'I've been looking for you all day.'

'Well, now you've f-found me,'

'How did you know I would?'

'I kn-know you.'

'Where were you?'

'Helping Mrs Gilbey, and other things.'

I feel Mrs Gilbey's hands on my shoulders. She kisses the top of my head. 'Happy birthday, my dear. Here, let me take your coat.'

I don't say anything, because I can't. I'd like to, but the words have got stuck in my throat. She goes across to the table and, like a conjuror, pulls off the white tablecloth. It reveals the fullest table I've ever seen. Sandwiches and cakes and jellies – so many different kinds!

'Those are fish paste, those are Spam, and over there there's cheese and tomato.'

Granddad gets himself a plate. 'Looks wonderful. Well, I for one am famished.'

I remember how hungry I am. Mrs Gilbey starts to cut the home-made fruit cake into slices.

'Come on, then. I don't want any leftovers.'

We fill our plates. Reggie moves over so that there is room for me next to him. 'Happy birthday.'

'Thanks.'

'Sorry about g-going missing, only there was a lot to do.'

'You're always going missing. Think I'll start calling you the invisible man.'

But I'm so glad. I feel as though I've been rescued from

something. Saved. A bubble feeling that might burst if I touch it.

Soon everyone is talking and laughing. Mrs Gilbey and Granddad talk about all kinds of things. The birthdays they had when they were children. What they did when they were young. Where they'd been. You can tell they like each other – they share the conversation, taking it in turns to talk and listen. They ask us questions the way older people do when they want to remember being young. Norman keeps telling jokes and talking about the war. I tell them a bit about my play, but mostly me and Reggie sit and listen. It's like we're both waiting for our time.

Mrs Gilbey puts on her wireless for a while, so there's music. There's not much left on the table now, except for a few pieces of cake and some sandwiches. Me, Reggie and Norman ate most of the cake first, while Mrs Gilbey and Granddad were eating the sandwiches. There's still a slice of bread pudding left. It goes quiet for a while, the way it does sometimes. It's a nice quietness, as if it's supposed to happen and no one feels the need to fill it.

I offer Reggie the last piece of bread pudding. He takes it. 'You're not s'posed to do that.'

'What?'

'Take the last piece.'

He grins. 'Someone has to.'

He's got a point. As usual.

'Why didn't you tell me about this?'

'Because it was a surprise. That's the point of surprises.

You surprise people.' He munches into the bread pudding. 'This is good.'

'You could've given me a clue.'

'You're the one who r-reads all the Sherlock Holmes books.' He finishes the pudding and licks his fingers.

Mrs Gilbey and Granddad are looking through a photograph album. Mrs Gilbey looks up. She shuts the album. 'I've got a little something for you, sweetheart.' She goes across to the chest of drawers, opens a drawer and takes out a small, thin parcel wrapped in blue tissue paper. She gives it to me.

'What is it, Emma?'

'Only one way to find out, dear.'

'Thanks.'

'You're welcome.'

I slowly unwrap the paper, trying not to tear it. Inside is a pen. Just like the one Sister Vincent has. It's beautiful. Green. With a 22-carat gold nib. I've never had anything like this before in my whole life.

'Blimey. It's brilliant . . . fantastic.'

'For you to write your stories.'

Norman comes over. 'You'd better take this.' Looks round suspiciously. 'You might need it. They never captured Hitler, you know. He could still be on the prowl.'

Granddad says, 'Not in Hawkins Street, though, Norman, surely?'

Norman gives the side of his nose a knowing tap. Hands me something wrapped in newspaper. I open it. It's a wooden rifle and a red balaclava. I wonder if he's thinking of starting his own army and I'm the first recruit.

'Thanks, Norman.'

'That's all right. I made it meself. Fires fifty rounds a minute. Lee Enfield. Best rifle ever made.'

'Thanks. It'll be really . . . useful.'

'S'what I thought. Can't be too careful. Me mum made the balaclava.'

'It's lovely.'

'Red. For a girl. No good on night patrol, though, you'd be a sitting duck.'

'Right.'

Granddad comes across. 'And this is from me.' He hands me an envelope.

Mrs Gilbey smiles at him and says, 'Just like a man not to wrap a present up.'

I open the envelope. Inside are two keys. I look at him, puzzled.

'It's the key to the piano, lassie. The other is the key to the flat. In case we're not there and you want to practise. We want you to have it. It's not worth much, but it can still play a sweet tune in the right hands. Oh, and don't worry, it can stay upstairs for as long as you want it to. Go up and play any time you want. There are some old music books there for beginners. They might be of some use.'

As I look at the little key on the blue ribbon, my eyes blur. I try to speak, but I know if I do I'll just start crying. I lean across and kiss him on the cheek.

Reggie gets up. Goes across to his coat hanging over the chair. Comes back carrying a small, oblong package. 'And I g-got you this.'

'Looks like a book.'

'Instructions on how to f-fire Norman's gun! Only kidding.'

'Wow . . . Sherlock Holmes.'

'It's *The Hound of the Baskervilles.*'

'Haven't read that one.'

'G-good.'

Norman looks over my shoulder.

''Ere, Al, Sherlock Homes, he's the bloke in our play.'

*Our* play. I like that.

'I've been learning my lines. Can't wait. My mum's coming to see me. She reckons that . . . Blimey, my mum! I forgot all about her. I said I wouldn't be long. Better get back. Thanks for the grub, Mrs G. Brilliant. I won't be able to eat for a week. See you two later.'

'See you, Norm.'

Mrs Gilbey gets up. 'Don't forget your balaclava, Norman, it's blowing up out there.' She turns to me, looking a bit concerned. 'Looks like it's going to be a bad storm.'

I pull a face, shrug my shoulders.

'Angus, would you take those plates out to the kitchen for me?'

They go out, still talking. Suddenly we're on our own, me and Reggie.

'Good b-birthday?'

'In the end, the best.'

He looks at me like the cat that got the cream.

'I've got s-something else for you.'

'What?'

He reaches into his coat pocket and pulls out an envelope. Looks like another birthday card.

'It's what I've been telling you about. It doesn't look m-much but it's p-probably the most important birthday present you'll ever have.'

'What is it?'

I slip my fingers inside the envelope. Peer in. It's not a birthday card.

'Be careful, it's a bit f-fragile.'

I slide it out of the envelope slowly. It's a photograph. I hold it out. Let the light play on it.

It takes me a while to take it in. To work out what he's showing me. It's my photograph but it's been joined to another one. It's not perfect; there's a ragged white line running through where the two halves have been joined.

'What is it?'

'Can't you see? It's the other half of your photo!'

I peer at it.

'It's a bit blurred Reggie. I . . . ?'

He interrupts, sounds excited.

'Look carefully.'

I do. Shadows pull across its surface. Tease my eyes. Shapes on paper. Light and shadow. Negative. Positive.

'It nearly fits perfectly. And see, you were right, the man in your half does have his arm around a lady and look . . . '

He sounds really excited like he's just discovered buried treasure or something

' . . . the lady is holding a baby too.'

He's right but I feel like I'm missing something. Being stupid. I look up at him. His eyes are bright.

'I couldn't believe it when you first showed me your half. I knew straight away it would f-fit my bit and it does, doesn't it?'

'Your bit? What d'you mean?'

There's something else in his voice now. Like he's just run the longest race ever and come in first. It's over and he's the winner.

'The other half is m-mine. I'm the other b-baby. I had the other half of the photograph. It was found with me. Just like your bit was with you. L-look at the man. Anything familiar about him?'

I peer at the face again. Turn it to the light. One minute you can see something, then you can't. I'm not sure what to say, but he doesn't wait for a reply.

'He looks like you, Alice. The same curly hair and your lopsided grin. You must be able to see that. It's your dad, Alice. Your real dad.'

The words spin in my head.

'My dad? My real dad?'

My stomach yo-yos but I force myself to take my time. Look carefully. Take in every detail of the photo.

'But if it is my dad, what's he doing with his arm around the lady who's holding you? This is bonkers, Reggie. I don't get any of it.'

'Wake up! I thought you were supposed to solve puzzles. It's a photograph of a family, Alice, and we're both in it . . . Part of the same family.'

He pauses, grins.

'Which means . . . '

He pauses again, waits for it to sink into my overloaded brain. And it does.

' . . . you're my brother?'

'Worse than that. I'm your twin.'

He looks a bit embarrassed, a bit happy, a bit shy, a bit pleased with himself. 'Well? What d'you think?'

He might just as well have asked me how many miles to Jupiter. I shake my head.

'I just don't know Reggie. This is too . . . '

My words trail away. I look at Reggie, then back at the photograph, and all of a sudden, for no reason, I'm sure. I want to shout and sing and dance all at the same time. Instead, I burst into tears.

'Hey, it's not that bad! And I j-just thought of something else. If it's your birthday and we're twins, it must be my b-birthday too.'

'Except it's not my real birthday. Mum called the day I was taken to the orphanage my birthday because no one knew when it really was.'

'In that case it can be my not-real-birthday too.'

'Happy not-real-birthday, then.'

I sit back down again.

'You all r-right?'

'Think so. I just can't take it all in.'

'It'll take time. Not every day you f-find you've got a genius for a b-brother. Still can't get used to having a little s-sister, come to that.'

'Not so much of the little.'

He keeps smiling. I just sit and let everything wash over me. Can't believe it. Us sitting here. The sound of Granddad and Mrs Gilbey chatting. The singing on the wireless. The firelight. I can hear Mrs Gilbey and Granddad laughing in the kitchen. They seem to be a long way away. On the wireless Big Ben chimes out the time.

I count the chimes. 'I'm gonna have to go, Reggie. I didn't realize it was that late. I don't want to get into any more trouble with Bert. I'll come up for you tomorrow. We've got a lot to talk about.'

From outside comes a distant rumble. Reggie goes over to the window. Looks out.

'It's still raining. Getting heavy. Think that's thunder. I'll c-come with you.'

'No, it's all right. I'll be fine.'

'You s-sure'

'Sure. I'll take the short cut by the old shelter. Won't take long.'

I can see the uncertain look in his eyes.

'I can take care of myself. Anyway, I've got a lot to think

about. I'll be better on my own.'

I get up, get my things together. 'See you later, then.'

He still looks worried 'You certain you're s-sure?'

'Reggie.'

'Sorry, it's not every day you get a sister. I don't want to lose you now.'

'Don't worry. I'm not going anywhere.'

'S-see you tomorrow, then.'

'Oh, and Reggie – '

'Yeah?'

'Thanks.'

# ★★★ 26 Facing fears

Outside the sky is all around me. Like it's wrapping me up. A spider's web of a sky, trapping me and my thoughts. The rain is heavy. Thunder rumbles somewhere in the distance. I walk quicker. There are two streetlights at the bottom of Lyndsay Street. They beacon out a glare of yellow light. Raindrops pattern the air around them. In empty doorways shapes move then fade as I pass them. Strange noises tease. Play tag.

'Sherlock, you there?'

'As ever, my dear.'

'Bit scary out here.'

'We'll be all right.'

'What a day.'

'You said it.'

'Got myself a twin brother. Didn't work that one out, did you?'

'Who'd have guessed it.'

'Right.'

'Looks like a bad storm coming, though.'

'Afraid so.'

I start to walk towards the old bomb site. It's a short cut

home. I've been this way hundreds of times before. But with every step I start to get a strange feeling in my stomach. Like something's not right. Something's telling me to stick to the lit streets. Keep away from the dark of the bombed ruins, the smashed houses, the secret shadows.

I start to feel uncertain. Strange. I know this place. Every part of it. Daydreamed away too many days, played too many games here to be scared. So why am I? Somewhere lightning crackles. I look up into a smoky, black sky. The storm is heading my way.

'Change of plan, Sherlock. We'll go back up Lyndsay Street then into Sidney Street. Long way round, but it'll be light all the way then.'

'Right behind you.'

Lightning tugs at the edge of the sky. I put my head down and walk as fast as I can. The rain drives at me. I pass the two streetlights, get to the bottom of Lyndsay Street, stop. Look down Sidney Street. It should be bright, well lit, but I stand looking into a long tunnel of darkness.

'Strange.'

'Mmm. Power cut? Might be the storm.'

'What d'you think?'

The rain is dripping from my hair. Tracing invisible lines down my face. Making queues at the end of my nose.

'Come on, let's go. Maybe the lights will come back on.'

I start to walk. Sidney Street's a wide street. Lots of factories. Many of them were hit by bombs during the war. Looking down the street now is like looking at a comb with half its teeth missing. Left over, left behind. In the gaps between the factories, broken furniture and rubbish is piled among the bricks and buildings. Prams without wheels. Twisted chairs, broken-backed tables.

'If we can make it to the bottom I think we'll be all right, don't you, Sherlock?'

'Sure to be.'

The storm is rolling in. I can feel it in the air. Heavy. Suffocating. It seems to be taking for ever to walk down the street. I feel tired. Maybe it's just all the excitement. Maybe I'm just scared of the storm.

One of the street lights flickers on and off. Above, a fork of lightning streaks across the sky, lighting up black clouds.

'Fancy a run?'

'Nothing like a bit of exercise. Bit of an athlete in my day, you know.'

'Bet I can beat you.'

'No chance, dear girl.'

I put my head down and charge into the sheeting rain. It clatters into gutters, waterfalls down drains. A racing tide. It's like running through a river, splashes up all over me. I'm soaked. The sky is dark. The street echoes to the booming thunder. I can't see a thing, except in the split second when lightning tears open the sky and shows me the black and white world. Still, I'll soon be home now. Only a few minutes more and I'll see Hawkins Street.

The loudest clap of thunder I've ever heard explodes in the sky. Rings in my ears. At the same time, the sky lights up and I can see everything. The factories. The street. But what I see confuses me. These are not the streets I know. It's as if someone's letting me see I'm lost. Laughing at me. But how can I be lost when I've lived round here all my life?

I've got to take shelter. I must have taken a wrong turn somewhere. Lightning conjures a tall building out of the darkness. I see it just long enough; it looks more or less intact. There's a sign over the door half hanging off, swaying. It has a name written on it. For some reason I look up at it.

'Westlands Metals'

'Seem to know that name, Sherlock, don't know from where though. Let's take shelter here.'

'Careful, Alice, these old bombed factories are dangerous places.'

I grab the door handles and pull them hard. The doors creak. The wind catches them and flings them violently open. I step inside and find myself standing in the shell of an old factory, the size of a football pitch. It's high and so dark, but in the flashes of lightning I put together what I see. Taking photographs with my eyes. Waiting for the lightning to develop them. Lots of broken windows – jagged glass in twisted frames. The remains of what was once the ceiling sags open dangerously, a ribcage of splintered planks and rafters hanging down. There's lots of rubbish piled up in dark corners – old upturned cupboards and desks, broken mostly, boxes piled against one wall, covered in dirt and rubbish. They look like they've been here ages.

Rain sweeps through the factory, trickles down on to the floor. I try to feel my way in, using the lightning strikes to see. In front of me is some kind of conveyor belt. I suppose once there would have been dozens of people sitting alongside it. Making things, checking them, putting them into boxes, stacking them. Now it's completely smashed. Probably bombed during the war. I don't see the twisted metal sticking out. Walk straight into it. It rips my dress, slices into my leg. I feel the trickle of blood.

Suddenly a crack makes me jump. Lightning forks down, spits in through a window. I duck, and in that instant of light my heart skips a beat. I can see someone across the space. Near the far wall.

I suck in my breath.

'Who's there? Who are you?'

The light goes. My voice rumbles around. Echoes back.

Nothing. Just shadows playing tricks. I'm imagining things again. The thunder seems closer. Booms at the building. The storm's overhead now. Lightning fizzes in again, heading straight for me. I duck. Fall to my knees. Scramble under the conveyor belt. Something hisses past, hits the ground, exploding into a fireball, setting fire to a pile of rubbish.

I look back across the space again. The fire bathes it in orange light. I peer through the smoke. There is someone there. I can see her clearly. I stare into the eyes of a girl. A girl I know. I wasn't imagining it. It's me. It's my reflection. My reflection in some sheets of metal leaning against the far wall, that's what I can see.

Another fork of lightning plunges through the dark. This time it hits the corner of the conveyor belt above my head. It bursts into flame. I can smell rubber burning. The fires are beginning to spread, sweeping across the factory floor. The doorway where I came in is a furnace of flames. The smoke choking. I'm not going to be able to get out that way. Sooner or later this building is going to collapse, with me in it. I know I've got to get out, but if I do I'll have to face the storm. It's almost as if I know it's waiting for me. I know that's stupid, but it's how it makes me feel. There's a terrible groaning noise. Across the other side of the factory, part of a wall collapses and some of the metal sheets clatter noisily to the floor. Above me the roof begins to creak. I wonder how long it can stay up.

Then I hear it. A scuttling black crow of a whisper. That familiar voice carrying on the wind. And the wind becomes his voice. Wrapping around me. It's like he's here. In the shadows. In the air. Playing games with me. A cat with a mouse. I edge away. Look up. Up and out through the roof. As I do a cloud rolls away, moonlight leaks cold, grey. Bits of the roof collapse and tumble down in clouds of wood, bricks and rubble and I remember his promise. 'A birthday surprise, just for you.' His words seep in through broken window panes, rattle against the frames. Something to teach me a lesson.

I'm frightened. I want to hide, to run away, to get out of this nightmare.

Somewhere a long way off, a dog barks. A simple bark in the night. Sounds like Flash. The thought comforts me and at the same time I get that feeling again. Like someone or something is there. A feather touching my face. I start to think and as I start to think I start to move. Step out of the shadows. My hair is in rats' tails and I can feel the blood hot and sticky on my leg, but somehow I feel stronger now. Something takes over inside me. An idea. A way to beat the fear. It's almost as if the storm is in me now. For the first time in my life I don't feel scared. I suddenly know what to do. I go across to the metal sheets stacked against the opposite wall. The metal that reflected back my face. I've got an idea.

I start to pile up the sheets. As I collect them I remember lots of things that have happened since Reggie came to live upstairs. The beatings, the worry about Mum and the baby, finding out I'm adopted, Flash being killed, all the things I've been trying to sort out. All those things that seemed to be pushing me down. Scaring me. But now I realize something. That I've got stronger because of them and I know that running away isn't the answer. I keep piling up the metal plates. I pile the metal higher and higher. It's a simple idea. It might work or it might not. But I have to try. Electricity is attracted to metal and I'm going to see if I can draw the energy to this one point, these metal plates, short-circuit it, burn out its power. Destroy it, and everything that's in it. All those bad memories. All that fear. I have to believe I can do it. I have to believe in myself.

The storm is all around me now. A roaring, tumbling mountain of energy. I can feel the electricity in the air. I'm ready. Now is the time. I hold my breath.

The air stills. The night stops breathing. The only sound is the slow drip of water. The fires burn soundlessly around me. I've done as much as I can. I stand, look up at the night. Wait.

In that moment of stillness I'm sure I see him. Clear as day. Dark as night. His face. Those grey eyes. Then I blink and he's gone and the lightning hits. A thick, crooked spark of pure white energy. On target. The force hits the pile of metal like a runaway train. I can feel its power. It hits and rebounds in a fury of light. The building trembles. Shudders. More bricks start to rain down. Bits of wood crash to the floor. What's left of the glass cracks and crumbles. The energy meets and mushrooms up, up and out through the roof in a cloud of fury. Red and yellow flames sheer off, the sky catches light.

Then comes the noise. A deafening roar, like the fire has burned a hole for the sound to pour into, to fill up. Angry.

Hard. A split second, then the full force of the blast hits me. I'm thrown back across the floor, into the wall, hitting my head on the cardboard boxes stacked there. They fall around me spilling their contents – hundreds of metal boxes scatter across the floor.

# ★★★ 27 Girl on a biscuit tin lid

Slowly, all the sounds fade. Murmur into silence. I'm lying on the floor. I try to move, but can't. Everything is calm. I ache. My head hurts and my leg is wet with blood. My dress is in tatters. But it's so quiet now. So peaceful.

Through the holes in the roof the moon slants in. Something on the floor in front of me catches the light. Slowly, I reach out. Pick up it up. It's a biscuit tin. That's the last thing I see as the walls of the old factory groan and stumble for the last time.

Who'd have thought it? I smile to myself calmly. Wood splinters and crackles all around. Bricks groan and topple and crash down. The roof creaks, leans at a strange angle, then tips slates down in a rain of dust. But amidst all this chaos, all I can think about is the little tin box I'm holding. Exactly like mine, except this one is brand new. They must have been made here. That's what the metal sheets were for. They made the biscuit tins here. And they were what I used to beat the memories, the fear, to beat the storm. I start to laugh. Laugh and cry at the same time. Tears roll down my cheeks.

I try to move again. Can't. But I don't care. My eyes are fixed, held by the picture on the tin because now, for the first time, I can see it clearly in fresh, bright colours. I'm looking at the little girl with the red hair. She does look just like me. She's in a field, sitting on a swing. The sky is so blue. The leaves on the trees so green. And for the first time I can see what it is that's on the floor close to the swing. It's like a tunic, the sort that soldiers wear. It's lying there like someone's just left it for a moment. But that's not all. There's something on top of it. I strain my eyes to see it. Can't make it out. It's so fine. So light. Barely a mark on the tin. A speckled trace of light. Looks just like a feather.

## ★★★ 28 Awake

The sun is golden syrup. It pours itself over my face, spreads itself on my closed eyelids. I try to open them. They move slightly, then butterfly open. I look around. Where am I? Close them again. Open them. Still don't know where I am. But there's a nice familiar smell. Soap and lavender. I'm not worried.

I try to sit up. Everything aches. Especially my head. That feels like it might belong to someone else. I put my hand to it. Out of the corner of my eye I can see a bit of something white hanging down. It's a bandage. I sink back down into the warm, comfortable bed. A door slowly opens.

'Alice?'

I peer through squinty eyelids. A face creased into a worried frown looks round the door.

'Emma? What you doing here?'

'I live here, dear. I thought I could hear you stirring.'

I try to sit up again. She comes further into the room. 'You be careful now. Here, let me get your pillows.'

'What happened? How did I get here?'

'Just rest. You've had a lucky escape, my girl.'

Slowly, my muddled head clears. I remember. Words tumble.

'It was terrible, Emma. There was this awful storm. I got lost. I went into an old factory. The storm came in and there was thunder and lightning everywhere and the whole building shook. But the storm kept coming, and I knew it was more than a storm. It was like it was after me. Looking for me.' A single tear curves down my cheek. I wipe it away. 'Everything burst into flames and I had to hide under this conveyor belt. Then I had this idea. and I stacked up the metal and . . . ' The words gush out. I can't believe I'm rabbiting on like this. But deep down I know what I'm saying will only ever make sense to two people. Me and Reggie.

Mrs Gilbey moves across the room. Plumps up the pillows. Then sits on the bed and puts a cool hand on my forehead. 'All right. All right. You can tell me all about that later. You need to rest now. No talking. You've got a temperature and a lot of bumps and bruises.' Her worried frown deepens.

I try once more. 'I've done it, Emma. Don't you see? I've done it. I've beaten it. No one is ever going to frighten me again. I have to tell Reggie.'

She gets up. Goes over to a small bedside table. Carefully pours something from a tall bottle into a glass. Then she comes back to the bed.

'You must calm down, young lady. You're a very lucky girl.' She looks at me. 'It was just a storm. The firemen got you out just in time. Such nice young men. One of them told me another couple of minutes and the whole building would have collapsed, with you in it. Two direct lightning strikes, he said. Worst electrical storm any of them had ever seen. And there were old chemicals in the factory. Apparently, they used to use them to colour the lids of biscuit tins. Dangerous stuff. Caught fire straight away.'

She offers me the glass. I realize how thirsty I am. Gulp at it.

'Slowly, take your time. He said the whole place was lit up like a Christmas tree.'

I realize we're telling two different stories. Two different stories to describe the same thing. I'm talking about the way I've faced my fears. She's talking about something ordinary – a bit of bad weather and some dangerous chemicals.

Questions start to dart through my mind.

'How long have I been here? How's Mum? And where's Reggie?'

'So many questions! Three days, your mum's fine, and I've no idea where Reggie is. But I'm sure he'll turn up when he's ready.' She pauses. 'I spoke to your mum – let her know what happened and that you were all right. She said to tell you the baby is due any day now . . . ' her words trail off.

'What is it? Something's wrong with Mum, isn't it?'

'No. There's nothing wrong with your mother. There is something you have to know, though. She said I should tell you.'

There's a look in her eyes. Like she's worried.

'This is probably the wrong time, but I don't suppose there will ever be a right one. Anyway, you have to know sooner or later, and you're a brave girl, you've proved that . . . '

She takes my hand. 'It's your stepdad. It was the night of the storm. He was out in it. Mr Higginbottom saw him. Said he was wandering about in the rain, soaking wet. Mr Higginbottom shouted to him to find some shelter but your stepdad said he was looking for you. He had to find you. Seems there was this terrible crash, fit to wake the dead and then, according to Norman's dad, the biggest bolt of lightning he'd ever seen shook the whole street. He said it was just like the sky was exploding. He ducked into a doorway and next time he looked out your stepdad was gone. Like he was never there at all. Gave Mr Higginbottom quite a turn, I think.'

She takes a deep breath. 'Your stepdad hasn't been seen since. The firemen and the police have been looking for him but there's no sign of him anywhere. It was up by those old factories, quite close to where you were found. Seems the fire spread to all of them. There's not much left. They're all gutted.'

She looks at me, waits for me to say something. I stare at the floor. Mrs Gilbey pats my hand. Her voice goes quiet,

'I know things haven't been so good between you. I suppose he just couldn't accept that you were growing up, changing. Some people react to that in the only way they know: by hitting out, by being violent.'

She looks at me.

'I'm not excusing the things he did, Alice, don't think that for one minute. I'm just trying to explain how it might have been.'

She takes my hand. Her hand feels warm. She reaches for the hanky that she keeps up her sleeve. Dabs at her eye. Sniffs.

'There, I've probably said all the wrong things. Stupid old woman that I am.'

I smile. Give her hand a squeeze

'You'll never be that, Emma.'

'Yes, well.'

'You all right?'

'Of course I am, dear. I'm just trying to find the right words. The right words for you.'

She looks around like the words she's looking for are floating in the air. Invisible. Waiting to be plucked.

'You know, often the things we hate most are the things we fear most. But the funny thing is, Alice . . . ' She puts her hanky back up her sleeve. Her eyes glisten. ' . . . sometimes what we're really afraid of is what's inside us. It's not out there at all but buried away deep inside, out of sight. It's just easier to put the blame for the way we feel on what is outside. Maybe what we're all so frightened of is just being frightened.'

She smiles and shakes her head. 'Now, that really is it.

I've said enough for one day. And in the end we all have to make up our own minds about life anyway. What it is, who we are, where we fit into it all.' She squeezes my hand back. 'It's those scientists and Indians again, darling. Scientists and Indians, eh?'

## ★★★ 29 The letter

The bump on my head must have been bigger than I thought. I drift in and out of sleep. Lose track of time. Watch the morning sun winking over the windowsill. The evening moon peeking out from clouds snow-banked high. Most of the bits in between get mixed up. Bits of daydreams and nightmares wander around together. I dream of Bert and the storm and the factory. I know that when I beat the storm, suddenly I wasn't scared of him any more, and I can't help wondering if it was my fault that something happened to him. Was he there at all that night or was it just my good old imagination again? Then I push all the wonderings away. Block them out. Think about Reggie. Where is he? Will we ever get to the bottom of all this?

Slowly my eyes get less heavy. The bump is less sore. The pieces of the story get put together in my mind. But they're almost as painful as the bump.

Mrs Gilbey comes in and out of the little bedroom. Visits to bring me food. Visits to see I'm comfortable. More visits to bring me more food.

Eventually, on one of her trips, I ask about Reggie again.

She folds her arms and frowns. Gets out her darning. Sits on the end of the bed and says, 'Eat that soup before it gets cold, dear.' She looks at me over the top of her spectacles. 'If you must know, they've gone.'

'Gone? Gone where?'

'Who knows? I was prepared to give that young man the benefit of the doubt. Thought he was just someone who needed a bit of help. But when I told him what had happened to you, well, he started all this nonsense about twins and mind-touching and heavens knows what else he was going on about. Then the next day they were gone. Seems to have spent his young life coming and going, that boy.'

She gives a little shrug.

'You have to wonder why, don't you?'

'You mustn't think bad of him, Emma. To him it was all true. Every single bit of it.'

'And to you?'

'Me? I know who I am now. That's all that matters.'

'You are a strange one and no mistake. Deep as the ocean.'

She pulls a face but can't stop the little smile peeping through. She looks at me over the top of her specs.

'He left you a letter. To be honest, I was tempted not to give it to you, but since he's gone I suppose it doesn't matter much. And before you ask the question, the answer is no. You can't have it yet. I'll give it to you when you're feeling better.'

'But I am feeling better.'

'You will be once you've eaten more of my soup.'

I pick up the spoon.

She gets up. Plumps up my pillows again. Kisses me on the forehead. Then she stands back, watching me eat.

'Finished?'

I show her the bowl. Lick the spoon for good measure.

'Now can I have the letter?'

She fishes it out of her apron pocket. Puts it on the bedside table.

'If things get too hard, you know you can always come here – if you want to talk about things, I mean.'

'I know that, Emma.'

She reaches out. Touches my cheek. 'One thing's certain, you're growing up fast, young lady. That's one thing I do know for sure.'

When she's gone I pick up the letter. I take a deep breath. Feel nervous. Open it.

*Dear Alice,*

*I hope you get this. We've left Hawkins Street. Going to be away for a few weeks playing detectives. My turn to be Sherlock Holmes.*

*I don't know what happened in that factory. Mrs Gilbey thinks you just got trapped in some old building in a storm. She thinks what you saw and heard was a lot of scary thunder and lightning. She's right . . . and then again, she's wrong. There's only one person who knows what that storm really was, and that's you. Mind you, I've got a funny feeling it was about you sorting things out. Sorting yourself out. I reckon the things that happen in real life sometimes are more scary and exciting than those that happen in mind-touching, or maybe they're two halves of the same thing.*

*I'm still trying to sort things out in my own mind too. Separate out what I know from what I've been guessing about. Sometimes things got a bit mixed up. I think your stepdad was jealous of you. Maybe he didn't actually mean to hurt anyone. It just got out of control. Jealousy is like that. Granddad said it's one of the deadly sins. Well, he said if it wasn't it should be.*

*Still, as long as you're all right now, that's the important thing.*

*I'm going to look for our dad now. Granddad's being trying to find any records that are still around. Seems a lot of stuff had been destroyed in the war, so there's not that much to go on. He found out from the hospital records that we were found in the ruins of a big house. You must have been found first. I wasn't found until later so I ended up in a different hospital. That's how how we got separated, I reckon. There were other records from that air raid. Next bit is a bit upsetting. Sorry to have to tell you like this but there's no other way. There was a woman found in the rubble too, but she died . . .*

I suddenly feel sick. My heart sinks. Two tears trickle down my cheek. I take a deep breath.

*. . . but there's no record of a man being killed during that air raid. That's something. I don't know where the photo came from or how it got torn. Maybe that's got something to do with*

*our dad and we won't know until we find him. That's the only way we'll ever get to the bottom of all of this.*

The door opens. Mrs Gilbey looks in. Doesn't say anything. I wonder if she thinks I've got Reggie hidden under the bed.

*Anyway, it's better if I do the looking; you've got other things to think about now. The new baby and that. Only thing is, it's not going to be easy. Like I said, lots of stuff was destroyed in the war. Lots of records lost. We've got one clue, though. The woman who was killed. Granddad went to the births, deaths and marriages place where they record all that. Her name was Mary Westland. If she was our mum, that must be our name too. Weird that, isn't it. Finding out what your real surname is.*

In my mind I see the old biscuit tin factory. The sign hanging over the door 'Westland Metals'. I read on.

*And Granddad said that piece of information should help us to find our dad. It's going to take a bit of a while, I expect, so I don't suppose we'll see each other for some time.*

*Right, I'd best be off. Granddad keeps shouting that we'll miss our train. Good luck, Alice. Thanks for being my best friend when I needed one. Hope I was yours.*

*Reggie*

I speak to the silence.

''Course you were, mate; the best friend ever.'

I sit there staring out of the window for a long time. I feel tired. My brain wants to think about all this. Sort it all out like a box of jumbled-up biscuits. Put each one in their right pile so that everything is how it should be. But I'm beginning to understand that real life isn't like that. I'm tempted to snuggle back down, go back to sleep, escape. But the stray rays of sunshine creep in over the windowsill. Through the glass I can see a deep-blue sky. A soft breeze ruffles the curtains.

I swing my feet over the side of the bed and get up. I've got a lot to do.

# ★★★ 30 There comes a time

I try to think about things here in my own small world. I think about school, the new baby boy that Mum had during the week, my play, my friends, how lucky I am. Even though I think of all these things, every time I walk down the passage I remember all the things that have happened and I look up and have to blink away the burning in my eyes.

Mum brought her baby home today. He's lovely. Chubby-faced. A down of dark hair. A blue-and-white bundle of gurgling bubbles. She's going to call him Albert, same name as my step-dad. Everybody says he looks just like him. Face off him, says Mrs Gilbey. Lots of people come to see him. They bring shawls, little boots and things. Why a baby needs boots is beyond me. Norman's mum has knitted him enough things to last until he's forty. Some of them look like they still might fit him then, as well.

Our little, damp, sunless room is sunny with laughter. Squashed with it. Babies do that, I think. I sit there watching them all. Don't know how I feel any more. A mixture, I suppose. Happy but there's a bit of sadness mixed up in it. Amid the chatter and the cups of tea I slip out. They're not going to miss me.

The air-raid shelter is empty. I pull back what's left of the canvas. Go to the little square of earth. Kneel down. Scrape away the top surface of dirt. It's there, in its hiding place, just as it always is. My old biscuit tin with its funny swirly writing and the background I can't see. Just a mix of colours. The one with the lid that won't close because my stepdad trod on it. Seems a long time ago.

I take it from its hiding place and open it. I could have had a new box from the factory. No one would have missed one. But this is the one I want. I take out the exercise book I bought from Woolworth's and the school pencil that I borrowed from school – Sister Vincent wouldn't mind if she knew what I was using it for. There's an old orange box in the corner that Reggie used to keep his comics in. I take it outside. It's a nice day. Sunny. I sit on the box, start thinking of all the things that have happened here. All the times I've sat here writing my stories. Sat here with Reggie.

And I wonder if the things we do stay around somehow. Do words wander the universe? Thoughts ghost the years? I get up. Pack all my things into the biscuit tin. I'm going to take it home now. I know I won't be coming back here, to the old air-raid shelter. I don't need to now. Maybe, as I pass by some days, I'll look across and think of things I did. Things I thought. But somehow, I know things have changed for ever.

I tuck my biscuit tin under my arm. It'll be safe now.

## ★★★ 31 Acting out of character

It's nearly the summer holidays. We're sitting on the edge of the playground, talking about the year that's gone, the summer holiday that's coming. At least, the others are talking. I'm mostly listening and thinking. Secret thoughts.

Veronica is bubbling away as usual. 'I think we're going to Seasalter. It's in Kent. My uncle's got a caravan there. It's great. We go looking for cockles at low tide. You have to walk very carefully and slowly, and keep your eyes glued to the sand.'

George looks puzzled.

'Why?'

She puts one hand to her hip, her 'I-can-see-I'm-among-fools' gesture. I'm getting to like it, in a funny kind of way.

'That's how you find 'em, dummy.'

'How?'

'Well, when you get near them, they know you're there and try to close their shells to protect themselves. When they do, a small jet of water shoots up. Not very high. Just a couple of inches. And you know that just under the surface is a cockle.'

George still looks puzzled but doesn't say anything. Josephine Murphy does. 'What d'you do with 'em?'

The other hand goes to the other hip. It's her 'not-you-too' stance. 'Eat 'em, stupid.'

Josephine pulls a look of disgust. 'Yuk.'

'No, not straight away. You boil 'em first.'

Josephine is unconvinced. The 'yuk' look stays on her face.

Norman starts going on about how he thinks they should make strawberry-flavour jelly to go with jellied eels. Veronica starts to look sick.

George turns to me. 'Wonder what Reggie's doing now? I liked him. He was . . . well . . . different.'

Veronica and Josephine continue to discuss cockles.

I say, 'Yeah. I miss him too.'

Veronica halts herself in mid-flow. 'Me too.'

I try to shrug it off. 'Come on, time for rehearsal. We're almost there now. It's getting good.'

Veronica says something about me being a slave-driver, but I know she doesn't mean it.

Sheila Morgan says, 'Most of us know our words.' I smile.

George gets this look in his eye. 'I've got a good idea. Why don't we invite everyone to come?'

Sheila looks uncertain. 'Everyone?'

'Yeah, not just the kids at Saint Michael's, but our own school, and parents too. We could even have it in our own hall. There'd be plenty of room.'

Veronica smiles at him. A cat that's got the cream. More people to be impressed by her acting skills. She nods. Likes the idea. So do the others. 'Fine by me,' I say.

As if she's just remembered something, Veronica says, 'Alice, you still haven't given us the words for the ending.' Looks at me. An accusing question. She sounds like Miss. 'You have *finished* it?'

I feel like teasing a bit. 'What?'

'The ending. We don't have an ending. You said you'd do it over half term.'

'Oh yeah. No, I didn't. Finish it, I mean. Couldn't think of a good enough way to end it.'

'But Alice, that means . . . '

I'm enjoying this.

'I didn't finish it. But someone else did.'

All eyes swivel to me.

'Who?'

'As a matter of fact . . . '

I take a long deliberate pause.

'. . . Norman.'

All eyes re-swivel to Norman. All mouths drop open.

George recovers first. 'But you can't hardly write a sentence, Norm.'

I smile my best secret smile. Norman says, 'Well, I can now, mate.'

Veronica looks at me sort of horrified. 'Is it any good?'

'Yeah, it's great. But you know the really strange thing?'

I leave the question teasing in the air.

Veronica says, 'What?'

'He said how easy it was. Didn't you, Norm?'

Norman seems to suddenly grow taller. He has the broadest smile I've ever seen on his face. His eyes twinkle.

''Bout as easy as falling off a swing, Al.'

I look at the others.

'What about that then?'

But no one says a word.

The night is a jumble. Bright lights. Shadows. On stage, acrobat words tumble. Veronica, George and the others juggle them. The audience laughs and applauds. I stand at the back. In the darkness. Look over their heads. Part of it all, yet separate from it. Two worlds. One real. One imaginary. The dark and the light. The question is, which is which?

As I listen, words become real. The characters I imagined – pictured – take shape. Not just in my head, but in the spotlight as well. Now Veronica and George are not my friends, they are Sherlock Holmes and Doctor Watson. They feast on the laughs. Grow fat with confidence. Unfurl the plot like a flag. Roll words like dice, daring the audience to guess what numbers they'll land on.

A few people laugh. Makes it all worthwhile. The play goes on. My mind flits in and out. One scene after another. The story unfolds.

Backstage, Gary rings his bicycle bell. Veronica picks up the cardboard telephone. '*Yes . . . yes. . . OK, put him on. It's the police for you, Holmes.*'

George takes the telephone. '*Speaking. No, not at all. No trouble. I'll do anything I can to help the poor people of Fiction Land. Go on, Inspector. I assure you I'm unshockable. Yes, Jack and Jill? Of course I've heard of them. They're refusing to do what? Go up the hill? Little Miss Muffet? Isn't she that delightful little lady who is so frightened of spiders?*' George puts this look of horror on his face. '*She's doing what? Pulling their legs off?*'

Veronica says, '*But Holmes, that's . . . homicide.*'

'*No, old friend . . . insecticide.*'

Lots of people groan. I join them, then remember I wrote it and go red in the dark. Characters come and go. Scenes change. I find myself thinking of Reggie again. Wish he was here to share this.

## ★★★ 32 The last bow

Then suddenly, like waking from a dream, it's the last scene. Gary and Denis sweep the spotlight on to the cast. The cast take a bow. Norman has a smile a mile wide. Doesn't look like Norman. Looks handsome. Not a knitted stitch in sight.

Applause rattles like rain. There are cheers and whistles. The hall lights come on. A sea of faces emerges from the dark. Mum. Mrs Gilbey. Just for an instant I think I see – no, it can't be. If only . . .

Proud teachers mumble thanks. My name is called. Heads turn. I smile, embarrassed.

Then it's all over, as if it had never happened. The audience drifts out in a scrape of chairs. Children discussing their favourite characters. Adults smiling. Thinking of the pub, or of other plays, long ago.

I make my way to the stage. Slip in through the curtains. Veronica, George and the others chatter amidst discarded costumes. Traces of make-up cling to red cheeks. Eyes are bright. We're lost in a shower of words, everybody getting wet at the same time. Ping-ponging experiences. Courting praise.

'I was rubbish.'

'You weren't, you were great!'

'Did you notice I forgot my words?'

''Course not.'

'Wasn't it good when they all laughed at the bit where Popeye jumps when he sees his own shadow?'

'Wasn't it a great ending?'

'Brilliant. Well done, Norman.'

'Denis was good on the lights.'

'Anybody check to see he didn't take them home with him?'

We all laugh. Sister Bernadette and Miss Lacey join us. Miss Druce is with them. Everyone starts talking at once again. Saying the same things. Shouting. Laughing. I smile and nod at all my friends. The reason I'm here.

Then, like snow in spring, they melt away. Drift off. Back to families. To homes. Talking of what was. What is. What will be.

It seems strange. The hall is empty now. The ceiling lights weeping weakly into dark spaces. Shadows cobweb the corners. Everyone's gone. I stand for a while in the silence and think. I call out my goodbyes to the empty space. Or *is* it empty?

Something moves in the far corner. The shadows part.

'Norman? What you playing at? I don't think that's funny . . . Norman?'

But it's not Norman. He leaves the shadow. Stands looking at me, that little grin turning his mouth downside up.

'Reggie? Reggie, it's you! Where've you been? What's

been going on? Why didn't you tell me you were here? Why didn't you come to the play?'

He smiles. 'We did. It was brilliant. We've been here all the time. Thought it was best to keep out the way until everyone had gone.'

'What d'you mean, we? Is Granddad with you?'

'No. I got lucky for once, Alice. Law of averages. Remember?'

He moves aside. Behind him is a man. The man nods at me and smiles. He has curly red hair just like mine but a bit darker and cut very short, and he looks at me with the puzzled, amused look of the man in the photo.

'I've brought someone to see you, Alice. Told you I would.'

The man takes a step forward. He holds out his hand awkwardly, as if he's not sure what to do. I walk towards him. Stop.

We stand there looking at each other for a few seconds. Then he smiles, and suddenly I know I've found my dad at last. My real dad.

I try to talk but I can't. It's as if thirteen years of words are all trying to get out of my mouth at the same time. I feel my body start to shake.

I'm so happy. But the silly thing is, the really silly thing is that I start to cry. And as the tears roll down my cheeks, my dad puts his arms around me and holds me tighter and tighter, the three of us close together in the darkness.